I0682176

BIGGER THAN THE BEATLES

Memories of a Dream Daffodil

Mike Simon

Edited by Tim Quinn

NEW HAVEN PUBLISHING LTD

Published 2025
First Edition
New Haven Publishing Ltd
www.newhavenpublishingltd.com
newhavenpublishing@gmail.com

All Rights Reserved
The rights of Tim Quinn as the author of this work, have been
asserted in accordance with the Copyrights, Designs and Patents
Act 1988.
No part of this book may be re-printed or reproduced or utilized in
any form or by any electronic, mechanical or other means, now
unknown or hereafter invented, including photocopying, and
recording, or in any information storage or retrieval system,
without the written permission of the
Authors and Publisher.

new haven

Copyright © 2025 Tim Quinn
All rights reserved
ISBN: 978-1-915975-15-7

To Jane, of course

And those wonderful supporting characters in my life:

The Noots, the Worleys, the Hawthornes, Greg Morris, Ash Bevan, Craig, Kaitie and all on the Carousel, Roag and Leigh and all who sail in the Liverpool Beatles Museum on Mathew Street, Paul Parry, Alan Cowsill, Lisa Thompson, Daniel Wiles, Fred Crampton, Wally Fitzgerald, Sister Dorothy, Sister Ethelreda, Pop and Lil, Mum and Dad, Rags, Grimm, Guss, Henry and Adrian

Email from BINK Publishing: Hi, Mike, Our highly successful series of biographies and autobiographies always kick off with a positive memory of meeting with a BIG name. Our readers love this. You've met the lot in your amazing career so pick the biggest and get me some words by Friday. We are all really excited by this.

Email from Mike Simon: Lennon was the biggest, but I met him when he was still smaller than Jesus. On that first meeting I found him to be a complete and utter knobhead but this was school rather than Rock days, and he'd just nicked my pack of Senior Service cigs, and my girl. Julie was her name. Now there was a star… (3000 words follow on Julie Cutler).

Email from BINK Publishing: Hi, Mike, We love the opening line but can we have more on Lennon rather than Julie?

TODAY

Today I came to the conclusion that I hate everything. Everything. That's a long trip to have made for the leader of The Dream Daffodils back in 1967. Of course, we all loved everything back then. It was easy. Everything was loveable. But today … I could feel it coming on walking up the stairs from Oxford Circus tube station. They hadn't even sent a car for me. Up to the BBC building as imposing as ever except it isn't. The dope on reception looked irritated by my presence.

'Yes?'

Fighting the urge to shout 'Don't you know who I am?' Instead, 'I'm supposed to be interviewed on Radio 1's Jason Barnaby show.'

'And your name?'

Fucking cheeky bastard.

'Mike Simon.' Not even a flicker of recognition or interest.

'Take a seat. I'll see if they'll see you.'

I sit and wait. Twenty minutes later than the time I'd been told to get there a ten year old walks up to me, checks his phone and asks, 'You Simon?'

I nod and he tells me to follow him. Corridors and 2 lifts. All the while the boy engrossed in the world of phone.

A friendly wave and urgent signal to sit opposite from Barnaby as we enter the studio. In t-shirt and torn jeans regulation dress code for BBC hip presenters, 'The Voice of the BBC' is gabbling a mile a minute to his FAB FM listeners. What he is saying is beyond me because of his speed and Godawful Brummy accent. Whatever it is, it sounds incredibly exciting so I guess we've landed on Mars or found a cure for cancer. He punches the air as he reaches the end of his claptrap with a Birmingham rebel yell and lets the latest tarty bird singer take over the airwaves.

'Hey, man! Good to see you. Who are you?'

Phone boy explains my presence.

'Oh yeah, of course. That's too exciting. You were with The Plantpot Men.'

'The Dream Daffodils,' I correct, visions of sugar plum Dalek extermination mingling with my Labyrinthitis.

'FLOWER POWER, MAN!' He bellows at me for no reason other than he's an idiot. 'We gonna have fun with you. It's a great day today. We've managed to get the rights to use vintage DJ Dave Lee Travis's famous jingle. You remember the one? WHACK-WHACK-OOPS!'

The noise brought back some memory of regular irritation but from where I have no idea.

'All we need from you is for you to read the words on this card,' Barnaby instructed.

I read them out. 'Infamy! Infamy! They've all got it in for me!'

'Thanks, man. That's great. You're good. One take wonder! Luke will see you out.'

'What about the interview?' I asked. 'You're supposed to interview me about the book.'

'What book? No, man. You're here just to take part in the Name That Voice slot. It should be weeks before anyone guesses it's you. Months even. Thanks again. See you. HEY! HEY! HEY! WE'VE GOT THE LATEST FROM JK TENDERMAN COMING UP..!'

The Barbers has always cheered me up. There's something so debauched about having someone fuss and tinker and act interested in your hair. And Jeremy is the best hairdresser I've found in over 60 years of searching. I should have known after the BBC puddings that the day wasn't going to get better. Another bloody receptionist shakes her head as I tell her my name and that I'm down for a 4pm with Jez.

'No, you're not. He's off. Cancer. Or Parkinson's. Something like that. Elsie can do you.'

I should have run, of course, but I was up for having my head washed, and by the time Elsie told me she was the trainee cum intern, she was already snipping.

'I like curly hair. Dead difficult to cut though. Easy to make a mess of it.'

She proved this with each successive slice. But I sat there for some reason believing she had a masterplan that would only be revealed at the end like a conjuror's trick. A three-piece suit sat next to me with a short back and sides and floppy top under which erupted an unkempt bush of a beard. I loathed him on sight and his voice grated in high pitched Cockney.

'I'd like to keep the overall look of a gentleman Viking.'

I knew I had to get out of there at once or risk violating my parole. I pulled off the hospital gown and handed it to the startled Elsie who followed me over to the counter, still attempting to snip away at my bollocks of a haircut.

'Don't you want me to blow you? You're not dry,' Elsie objected as I threw notes at the receptionist and hurried from the salon determined to get a lot less dry before heading home.

Overly cheery message on my phone when I staggered in after midnight. Agent Orange as I call her, or Gloria O'Range Media as she calls herself. She was very happy with my bit on the Jason Barnaby show. "Worked wonderfully well, luv. Twenty callers didn't get it. Let's make the most of this. We're on a roll. Coffee tomorrow at eleven. Usual place." The perfect end to a lovely day as I threw up in the kitchen sink.

Any cab company who puts a brick wall between passenger and driver will make a fortune.

'I'm not a racist, but...' was how this guy started. The but proved to be the usual problem of 'them coming over here'. The keynote in his speech was the line: 'I don't mind them coming here and being surgeons but I draw the line at them coming over and being taxi drivers.' He then took me into his confidence. 'The reason we're in the mess we are is that Boris Johnson. We were all fooled by him.'

I like the we. It worries me a bit that from as soon as I entered the cab the driver had me marked as a fellow far right card carrying klansman. I would have thought that any image I have would be more likely to be taken for lefty libtard snowflake. I blame the elocution lessons hoisted upon me at St Mary's College back in 1954 when I went from Liverpool "Y'wha?" to "I say, you fellows!" Blundellsands toff.

Orange was on her third latte when I walked in to The Coffee Shop just off The Strand. She was talking a mile a minute in German to two young girls who sat opposite her. They had matching candy floss hairdos, one Penelope pink and the other Grungey Green. They were attractive in a pinched German teenager way. Two guitar cases cluttered the aisle next to them.

'Don't scream, girls, it's the man himself!' warned Orange spotting me. 'Mike, say hello to The Bach Sisters.'

Mila was the pinko, while Lena was the greeney. They turned on me with identical wide smiles that remained too long for comfort. They were either nervous or the fanatical side of fandom.

'How are the bookings going for the tour?' I asked.

'Just great, luv, just great. How far have you got with the book? The publisher would love to see some pages.'

'How great? How many gigs and which venues?' It's not that I didn't trust Orange. Well, actually it is that I didn't trust Orange. After all, she was an agent, even though a strange one in a field of strange ones.

'You know how it goes. Softly, softly catchee monkey. But we have to make sure your autobiography is ready for release to coincide with the tour. So how far along are you?'

It was obviously a case of mutual distrust.

'Give me a week. Mutual exchange. Tour dates and bio.'

'Fantastic! Now you know that Granny flat of yours?'

'It's a connecting studio flat, Orange. My grannies have both long gone.'

'Can you do me a huge favour and let the girls kip there for a day? A week at most. I'm putting a tour together for them and they are a long way from home.' The girls hadn't stopped with the rictus grins since I sat down.

'I don't know…it's not that big a place.'

'Really it would be no longer than a fortnight until they are off.' Mila reached in her guitar case and handed me a CD and a

8

t-shirt both bearing the same image of the sisters looking like an advert for suburban hairdressers.

'Okay, a few days.' The girls both leaned over to hug and smile ever wider at me.

'Too, too kind. And this is our Mother and Father,' said Lena indicating a middle-aged couple sitting across the aisle.

PRE-HISTORY

It's that between Christmas and New Year time and what's left of my mind travels back to places I remember though some have changed. My very earliest memory at age 2 and 3 quarters was of traveling the 2 miles from my birthplace in Waterloo, Liverpool to what would become my childhood home in Blundellsands. It was a glorious village of eccentric Victorian and Gothic mansions, churches, gardens and people. Our own pile was called Park Corner and had been built in the 1870s by an architect for his own family. He didn't skimp and the house and grounds were overflowing with nooks, crannies and general oddities. Despite its size it was warm and friendly and instantly welcomed us. We were home.

The year was 1943 and history was all round us in Blundellsands. Two old Victorian gents would come carol singing at our door every 18th of December. They told us they had been visiting the house each year since they were boys in the 1880s! The were the real deal with waistcoats, scarves, fob-chains and pocket watches, pre Lennon tin rims and walrus moustaches. Dad would invite them in for a tot by the roaring fire. For some unknown reason they stopped coming after 1953. I can't think why.

My very first school, a convent, was in a castle a couple of streets away from our house. Although education, especially Catholic education, seemed like a terrible idea to me, I couldn't help but be impressed by the bleeding statues, battlements and forbidden oak doorway that schoolboy legend claimed led to the nuns' own dungeon. There was also a huge washhouse in the school grounds from which steam would always be hissing. Occasionally the door would be open and a nun could be seen stirring a huge vat of God knows what with a wooden paddle. One of the nuns taught me to spell the word 'elephant' which came in handy when I wrote 'Elephant Love' for the Wildlife Fund years later. Another nun showed me the exact location of my soul (just behind my forehead in front of my brain). That's not come in handy at all so far.

Our garden was full of trees and my favourite was one that had a branch that stretched over the perimeter hedge. I could lie on it, unseen, and watch people passing by on the pavement ten feet below. There was a blind man who lived nearby. He didn't wear dark glasses and his sunken eyes seemed mysterious and slightly spooky to this young boy. Even more mysterious was the fact that he ran everywhere, cane stretched ahead of him, whipping side to side, snakelike. Once he came to a sudden stop under my branch, sniffed the air and looked up directly into my eyes. "Hullo!" he said before racing off again. At some point he got a guide dog and the two of them would race around the neighbourhood.

A short walk away was a sweet shop named Confectioners. Dead posh that. Inside was the penny counter with every type of delight ready to be claimed by clutching paw. Above this counter sat a parrot on a perch. Didn't do me any harm as far as I know. The shop was run by Beryl who had been at school with my Mum. Beryl had a dark secret according to Mum. She never told me what it was, just that it was 'dark'. We should all be so lucky.

The River Mersey was at the bottom of our road. I could watch the steady traffic of shipping go by from my bedroom window with a powerful telescope we had inherited. You actually felt you were on deck.

In those early days our postman would break off from his round to sit in our porch and eat his breakfast sandwich, generously throwing crusts out to birds who would be waiting his daily delivery just as much as us.

At the top of our road was the Blundellsands & Crosby railway station connecting Liverpool to Southport. We were the midpoint on the route at Liverpool 23. Although a little station it had all mod cons with a magazine and booksellers and a waiting room with roaring coal fire in Winter months.

Directly across from our house was a key park with hills, valleys, woods and gorse that could cook a child when it had its bi-annual conflagration. The thick smoke would darken our neighbourhood. Dad used to head into the park at dead of night round Christmas time to come back with holly branches to coil up our staircase. The whole of Blundellsands looked its best when show fell with perfect timing during each Christmas week.

What can I say to sum up? I know I'll never lose affection....

YESTERDAY

I don't know what I was doing until April 6th 1957 but I certainly wasn't listening to music. It didn't help that we had no telly until later that year, and Dad only ever had the radio tuned to the Home Service. Not a lot of music there unless you count The Archers' theme, and that certainly didn't rock me Daddy-O. April the 6th is tattooed in my memory like Kennedy, Lennon and the Twin Towers but for sheer ringing joy rather than horror. I was sixteen and already dressing and getting the short back and sides haircut like Dad. He finally had a good job as a sales rep for Rowntree & Co., who had given him a brand new Morris 1000 to run around in, although ever since Suez there was word it might be replaced by a scooter. This seemed unlikely as there's not a lot of room for chocolate samples on a Vespa. Anyway, it had been tough for Mum and Dad for a long time so this period of calm was welcomed and they could see no better route for me to follow. Nor could I, until April 6th 1957. I was round Sinnott's house and we were making javelins at the kitchen table there. I don't know why we were making javelins, we certainly weren't sporty in the least. Probably some deep seated primal teenage instinct coming to the surface in response to the mumbo-jumbo Catholic schooling we were enduring each day under the Irish Christian Brothers, a teaching order just short of the Gestapo in their enlightened approach to education. I can see the coal fire roaring away and hear the kettle whistling on the stove. I can even see the red tiles across the floor and Sinnott's dog, Blackie, chomping on a bone. Life as we knew it. But it would never be the same again for me.

I don't know what the programme was, we had our backs to the telly at the time. Might have been *Tonight* with Cliff

Mitchelmore or maybe the *Six-Five Special*. Neither programme had ever caught my interest before when visiting friends or relations. But that changed this night. It was from the first note, like a herald angel from on high except it was the more nasal Lonnie Donegan. I swung round and my life changed watching his extraordinary performance. I was born again in that two plus minutes of jet propelled music. It was the attitude too. My God! His lead guitarist was actually chewing on TV! And Lonnie repeated the words Cumberland Gap 46 times in 123 seconds. Doesn't sound like much to you? You have to realise this was the Fifties and we were still living in rubble from World War Two. This was cosmic.

There was an earlier encounter with the entertainment world. It was Boxing Day 1948. I was eight and had been given a puppet marked on the box as the children's character Just William. Didn't look anything like the illustration in my favourite series of books but it was a puppet and that caught my imagination. It was a very snowy Christmas that year and I remember taking him for a walk round our house and being delighted at the two sets of footprints we left behind. I can still picture his little wooden shoes. Now that's a real toy, bugger your X-Box shite.

But 1957 was the year. By the time of my birthday in September I pooled together all the half crowns and ten shilling notes from my aunts, uncles, grandparents and parents, and sent it all off in a postal order for a 'Just Like the Professionals' guitar advertised in the back of *Titbits* magazine. I don't know who the professionals were who used this thing but when it arrived it left something to be desired. Horrible shiney paint job, Made in Hong Kong stamp on the back and the legend 'Just Like the Professionals' printed on the front. I attempted to paint the whole guitar from a leftover can from our living room but it honestly didn't help and I noticed a slight warp to the whole thing the following day. I took it into school and asked our music teacher, Mr Flood, for tips on getting started. He gave me a couple of lessons at the end of which I had mastered finger-picking 'London's Burning'. Not quite what I'd got a guitar for in the first place but it was a start. By chance or cosmic design, I hit upon the obligatory 3 chords necessary to become a recording star of the day, just fiddling around while lying on my bed tuned into Radio Luxemburg. Belated thanks to Horace Batchelor.

It was at a Christmas party that year that I met Richard Macadam. The rest, as they say, is history. Together we'd go on to conquer the world but on 18th December 1957 we were only interested in conquering Helen Fletcher from Merchant Taylor's Girls. The party was in St James Church scout hut up the tracks in Birkdale. I wasn't in the scouts but I'd heard Helen and a few of her Girl Guide friends would be there so I lashed out on the 6d rail fare. Could have gone on the bike and saved the dough but by this age I was already conscious of the quiff, which didn't take to the high winds of Hightown.

As I walked up to the church I saw Richard getting out of a taxi. Bloody typical. His family had money. They ran 6 pubs across Merseyside. I knew him by sight from school. He was in the year ahead of me. He looked cool...even in the school uniform. I never mastered that. It's funny thinking back to that meeting at the church gate. We would go on to be best friends, songwriting partners, deadly enemies, and back to best friends again in the years ahead. I think I can safely say that Richard is the biggest utter bastard I have met in my life. I love him to this day.

He had a guitar case with him and an amplifier. First I'd ever seen. He was dressed all in black, topped by the most perfect, well-groomed jet black quiff. Very effective in the falling snow. Rumour had it Richard was the most sought after boy at St Mary's by the camper of our teachers, and I could see why. You wouldn't call him handsome, he was beautiful. That's why we photographed so well together. His beauty and my more rugged, cheesed off look.

The Guides weren't on the look out for rugged that night. As soon as Richard entered the scout hut, I was pushed aside as the giggling troop converged on him with homemade scones and Dandelion & Burdock. By the time he had plugged in and played 'Santa, Bring My Baby Back to Me', it was game, set and match. Helen was his and the Vestry was christened as never before. I was both pissed off and impressed on the train home. I knew one thing for sure though, I wanted Richard Macadam in my band. Fucking bastard!

TODAY

'Utter twats! Tell me we never looked like those gobshites?'
asked Richard. We'd just stepped from the plane at John
Lennon Airport and there to meet us was the Mayor, a few
fellow council dopes, and a group of four young men dressed
to look like The Dream Daffodils at the height of Flower
Power.

'Somebody in Liverpool must be doing a roaring trade in
crap wigs.'

After handshakes with the mayor, the foursome surrounded us
and went into wacky poses as one of them threw bunches of
daffs and grinned like maniacs for the snapping cameras.

'Fer fucks sake,' objected Richard. 'Whose the fat one
supposed to be?' Luckily, our lookalikes got in a separate car
but we were still stuck with the Mayor and his wife as they
followed us into the city's Rolls. The usual draggy Lord Mayor
and wife conversation took place as we headed into town. Took
me back to ten thousand mayors and city dignitaries we'd been
lumbered with across the world during the time of the hits.

'Must be nice coming back home, boys?' asked his
Lordship.

Richard snorted and I found myself back in defence mode.

'Amazing. Can't believe you're putting up statues to us.'

'You've done so much for the city,' beamed Mrs Mayor.

'A lot more than the city ever did for us,' said Richard,
busying himself in rolling a joint. This day was going to be fun.
Why on earth we ever agreed to come back, I'll never know.
Bloody statues for God's sake!

I'd never been to a statue unveiling before so it's hard for me
to judge quite where on the statue hit parade ours would sit.

They had chosen an odd site to plonk us. The first floor of St George's market, just above the toilets. I suppose we might have played there at some time, the memory's not what it was sixty years back. The four lookalike tossers were already there as our party arrived. They were posing for more photos with the press. Don't know why we bothered coming really. Richard's shit must have been prime as he was well off his face now, with one arm round the Mayor's wife, his hand just a little too close to her right breast.

The crowds stretched to the far end of the mall on both floors and a cheer went up as we were spotted. Stupid but I still get a kick out of that. The cheer broke off into an even louder WAHEY as Richard lobbed a huge chunk of hash down to the ground floor. I know he was hoping for a fight to break out but luckily the Liverpool spirit took over and the slab was shared amongst various potheads.

I stood alongside Richard as the Mayor raised a hand and began the usual speech: Liverpool boys turning on the UK and then the world and then reinventing themselves for each successive generation. The films, the albums, the charitable events, even the three break-ups got a mention. 'What a fucking load of bollocks,' Richard breathed in my ear. And so it was, but I've heard longer tributes so give him his due.

We were asked to come forward to pull the veil to reveal our monument.

'Better not be the bloody Beatles under here!' bawled Richard to enormous laughter. Good and well timed gag considering his condition. Zip went the curtain and there were our 1967 selves stuck in time forever more. Or, at least until the market closes down, which, under the current government, could be in the next year.

The press honed in.

'What do you think, boys?'

'Very nice,' says I, very nicely.

'Why are there only four of us?' asked Richard. 'There were five of us back in '67.'

Typical. He always takes delight in bringing up Fifth Daffodil Laurence who is still serving time at her majesty's pleasure.

Titter from the press.

The dinner was pretty good. They'd gone to town at St George's Hall and turned the main room into a rezzy for the night. Rich mob turned up, probably funding God knows what in the back corridors of the council. Luckily, Richard had disappeared when North West Tonight's Annabel Tiffin turned up for an interview. Usual questions. Usual answers. Threw Mum and Dad in for authentic Liverpool cornball moment. Dad would have agreed with Richard on the whole thing being bollocks but I've always found my role in the Simon/Macadam partnership to be conciliatory, and so, for the sake of giving the public what they want, I informed Ms Tiffin that dear old dead Dad would have had a tear in his eye this evening. Yeah, right! A guy from the Echo turned up at the end of the night and asked me if we had a press release and photos. FFS as they say in Phoneland.

God knows what the pudding was but my gut was playing up all the way back to London. Richard had been spaced during the whole flight but as we parted at the airport he suddenly ran back and handed me an oval shaped deadweight wrapped in the Liverpool Echo and a ton of sellotape. The car was heading through Richmond before I got all the wrapping off and found myself sitting with my own statue's head in my lap.

As I walked in through my front door, I was greeted by the lead guitar opening to Lennon's Revolution shaking the rafters. A discordant drum solo was accompanying the racket. The fucking Bach Sisters were still in residence. I walked into the main hall, dropping my decapitated head with a thud on the oak tabletop. The girls played on oblivious as their parents, Helga and Joseph, filmed and recorded respectively. Computer screens, wires, mixing desk and amps had turned my baronial hall into a sodding recording studio. As the song came to its orgasmic conclusion, the Fourth Reich noticed my presence

19

and hurried over, all Aryan beams, hugs and braids. My stomach got the better of me.

'Still here?' I asked, heading off to bed in the furthest bedroom.

YESTERDAY

If you read the histories of British Rock and Roll, you'd think there had only ever been one Garden Fete in Liverpool. From May onwards every year since World War One there were hundreds of them. Any street with a garden would have a fete in aid of one thing or another. Always the same old junk entertainments, tombola, old book stall, lucky dip barrel, win a coconut, tea and cake stand, and raffles galore. Inevitably someone would get up and sing or dance or tell jokes.

Our first proper gig was at a garden fete. It was just the three of us. Me and Richard on guitars and his mate Laurence on stand up piano. Saturday 17th May 1958. Let that date be carved in stone forever more. There should have been six of us but Rob, Dennis and Derek on tea chest bass, washboard and banjo didn't bother turning up despite the 3 rehearsals we'd already put in. Richard and I made an on the spot executive decision, 'They're out!'

Laurence had wanted us to do the fete at the local children's home, which should have set off early warning signals, but, instead, we opted for the Unwed Mothers Home near Crosby railway station. I knew the place well as I'd often got wheels from their old prams for my soapbox-carts there as a kid. We got there early and took down nappies from a washing line to hang a white sheet to act as our backdrop. By the time all the stalls were set up we were between the books and the tombola. We were still three band name changes away from The Dream Daffodils back then. In fact, we hadn't even stopped to think of a suitable name for our band until Miss Straw, the manageress of the unwed mums asked us how we'd like to be introduced. Not wanting to seem as unprofessional as we were, I said the first word that came into my head. And so we were announced as The Crosbies that day. We played for fifteen minutes until we came to the end of our repertoire and then we looped back to the start and played the same songs over three more times. The audience reaction was to walk on by on their way to either the books or tombola. But we did get one of them. While playing Cliff's *High Class Baby* our final song for the final time, one of the unwed but imminent mothers burst into tears. I turned to Richard who beamed and nodded. Back of the net or what?!

10 years later to the day
Friday 17th May 1968
The Oz Magazine interview with Dream Daffodils Mike Simon and Richard Macadam.

MS: It's like I was saying the other day, you can look at something like a table, for example, yeah, like this table here, but that doesn't really make it a table, does it?

RM: Exactly. Because that's just words, man, just words someone dreamed up probably a thousand years ago.

MS: Yeah or in Victorian times or something.

RM: Well it would be before Victorian times. Tables have been around a lot longer than Victorian times.

MS: Y'think? Anyway, it needn't even be a table, like it could be this wall or this ceiling.

RM: They've still been around longer than Victorian times. This is a pretty old building.

MS: That's really not the point. You're missing my point. The point is....er....the point is like...er...I mean it's like whatever we say it is at any time in history. So that means nothing is really what we say it is.

RM: Yeah, it's just words, man, words.

MS: Exactly. Words are pretty meaningless. And that's what the new single was going to be about but we somehow got sidetracked in the studio and it ended up as something different.

RM: It's still meaningless though.

MS: Well not really.

RM: Yeah, I mean the words like. They don't mean anything when you break them down. They're more like a breeze, y'know?

MS: Yeah, a breeze or a ringing phone. You know like in a dream when you hear a phone ringing and you're running through your house but you can't seem to reach the room where you keep the phone.

RM: And then there are the dancers.

MS: They're great. We brought them over from Russia. Red Army dancers. Amazing. There were protests outside the studio that we were using Russians instead of British dancers but it's all one world, y'know. They were great. You can kind of hear them in the background during the bridge. Little feet going like the clappers.

RM: Gives a real different vibe to the record cos you know they're there.

MS: It was either them or Lionel Blair and his mob.

RM: Yeah or the Young Generation. (laughs for five minutes)

MS: Have you finished? The B-side is different. We wanted to try and capture the feeling of drowning. Just slipping further and further under water but relate it to falling in love. I nearly drowned once at Butlins so I could pull on that memory. It was horrible. The drowning not Butlins.

RM: We brought in weird wind instruments from the Tudor period. They give a real eerie sound especially against our triple tracked vocal loops.

MS: Next? We're off to do Frost's show in the US tomorrow but when we get back we'll be finishing up the album. *No Name Yet.*

RM: That's the title of it.

MS: And then the film.

RM: Oh fuck! I'd forgotten about that.

TODAY

Like my taxi driver, I've never considered myself racist. Human racist maybe. And there was that time in Wales back in 1955, but that's the Welsh for you. This morning, I wasn't even fully awake when I realised my hackles were rising. I'd never really been aware of the placement of my hackles on my body until I was brushing my teeth and found them vibrating up and down my back. It was the high-pitched sound from outside the bathroom door of Lena and Mila jabbering at speed. I could somehow hear the smiles in their voices and it pissed me off for some reason. Didn't help that they both hugged me good morning as I left the room. All that bloody hair dye is way too bright at that time of the day. They've got to go!

'They've got to go!' were my first words to Orange when we met in the reception of BINK Publishing two hours later.

'I know, luv, I know. Don't fret. It's all coming together. They'll be off on tour before you know it. And your tour is really coming together. Let's get this chat with Vincent over and we'll have a catch up coffee.'

Vincent is BINK. He looks like a rube from an American carny. Really knows how to fill a door frame. I don't think I've ever seen him not perspiring. Think Sydney Greenstreet having eaten Peter Lorre. Creepy bloat. Made his money in top shelf nauseous porn (*70 And Over, Crack Addicts' Cracks, Ugly Wives*, etc). He loves me and has every album and film.

'Looking good, baby!' His usual greeting and hug leaving a stain on my white shirt. Tea and biscuits poured we sat round his thirty-foot boardroom table.

'Loving the book so far but....we need more dirt. You know what the public wants these days. Just this side of filth. Enough with the Fifties stuff. There aren't enough readers still

24

alive from that period. Give me the Glittering Seventies up. Laurence's story. And anything on Saville, of course. Jim sells. We've just bought that *Playgirl* spread you did in 1973 so give us the story on that. We'll put it in as a *Big in the Seventies* centre page fold-out.'

Another half-hour of this non-stop rattle, Orange taking notes along the way. Always a relief to get away from Vincent. Coming down in the lift from his 25th floor ivory tower, I always get the feeling I should get an STD test. The wonderful world of publishing. As we headed across the road to Coffee Grounds, Orange handed me her neat 6 pages of notes. She'd even stapled them together. I dropped them in the handy litter bin outside the shop.

What can I say about Orange, keeping in mind she will read this. She's irritating, pushy and single-minded, which are all the things you need in an agent/manager. I'd probably be vegetating by now if it wasn't for her. I'm not sure that's any recommendation. Orange is small, that's the first thing she told me about her company when we first met one year ago. That was refreshing as all I'd had for the past fifty years were management companies telling me how big they were.

'I'm not Warner Brothers,' were her exact first words. Now that is a recommendation. She's in the business for the same reason I jumped on board back in 1957. Escape and excitement. Oh, and the birds. She does like the birds. Orange has a lot of heart. She cares about her acts and even advises them all to get rid of the agent and manager as soon as they can. But she is bloody irritating. I brought this up, sitting over Coffee Grounds coffee.

'You've got to get the bloody Bach Family Singers out my home, Orange! They're driving me nuts.'

'Why don't you like them? They're lovely girls.'

'You're not living with them and their bloody parents. I don't know why but they creep me out. Fucking hair dye splattered all over my shower and bathroom sink. And they're young!'

'Ahh!' said Orange like some amateur Dr Freud.

'Don't bloody say it like that. I've not just revealed my inner struggle. I don't like young people. Never have. Didn't like myself that much when I was young. But at least we had style not hair dye. I like to go home, lock the world outside and be on my own, not with the Fourth Reich.'

'A few more days, luv,' Orange crashed her mug against mine, spilling latte over my muffin. 'Just a few more and then big things will be happening for them and you. Can't say any more now but you'll be the first to know as soon as the final i and t are dotted and crossed. Friday at the latest.'

Bloody irritating woman.

Make that women. Back home Mila and Lena are on me as soon as I enter the front door.

'Big huuuug! We love you soooo much and we have great news!' I swear they said the words in close harmony. Mum and Dad beamed on from across the hallway, sat as ever at their computer screens, tinkering with the Bach Sister sound.

'Our single from last year has been picked up by a radio station in Brazil and they are playing it all the time.' Their excitement bounced off the walls and back again.

'That's fabulous, girls, well done.' I have no idea why I answered like that. I blame my Mum and Dad for insisting on a level of politeness at all times. Closing the door to my office, the real me shone through.

'Fuck 'em!'

YESTERDAY

Brazil radio for God's sake. We all have to start somewhere, I suppose. For all the newspaper, magazine articles and books written on us, I don't think any of them come close to recording the number of false Big Break starts our band had. Lenny the Lion was an early one. And that was TV, which was massive back then. Although it was a children's programme, it was sheer luck and sex that got us the gig. We were going under the name The Clickettyclacks (don't ask) at the time and we'd brought in an out of town saxophonist called Dudley Steven. I always liked the sax and would often try and bolster up our songs with it, so Dudley seemed like a good signing at the time. As it turned out, he was in the middle of a passionate fling with a producer in children's television so it worked even better than planned.

Lenny the Lion was as big as you get for a ventriloquist act. There were toys, board games, comics and even records from Lenny and his strangely plastic-faced human partner, Terry Hall (not of Fun Boy Three). We had our third single out at the time and it felt like real make or break time as the last two hadn't even dented the Hit Parade. One appearance on *Pops and Lenny* could change all that.

The show was recorded at the old BBC Television Centre doughnut in White City, so it meant a trek down to London, no easy thing due to a lack of motorways at that time and the state of our Commer van. I insisted we leave two days before the show knowing a big end or clutch box could drop at any minute. And so it came to pass as we were taking a long cut, due to Richard's map reading skills, through that hell on Earth, Birmingham. We were in our stage clothes for the simple reason that that's all we had at the time, and didn't fancy attempting to do battle with the innards of the van. We had a whip round and found we had £3.5s.3d. between us. More than I would have thought. Dudley said he'd sort it and disappeared while the rest of us spent 6d each on a cuppa.

Half an hour later, Dudley was banging on the café window, waving for us to hurry up and join him outside. Grabbing our instruments from the van, he led us round the corner and over to a car park at the back of the town hall. Ushering us towards a huge black Rolls Royce, Dudley threw open the boot and nodded for us to dump our instruments inside. Running round to the front, he had the engine running in seconds. We piled in and with a very un Rolls Royce screech of brakes we shot from the car park and hit sixty on two wheels as Dudley took us on the fastest route out of town.

'So you got this for £3?' I felt one of us should ask.

'Not exactly,' smiled Dudley, somehow lighting a fag and steering a zig-zag course as we put Birmingham behind us.

It helped turning up at the BBC in a Rolls. The guy on the gate was very 'yes-sir-no-sir-carry-your-bags-sir' from the moment we arrived. Big excitement in reception as we spotted Cliff Mitchelmore and Jack Warner chatting together. Showbiz didn't get bigger than that in 1963. The wonders continued as we were shown to our dressing room which had 100 watt bulbs all round each mirror. We'd never looked so unhealthy. Lenny and Terry popped in to introduce themselves, which was nice. Lenny looked even more motheaten than on the telly.

We got our first acting job on Lenny's show. Dudley's friendly producer, Monty, rolled in our costume rail. Apparently Lenny had invented a time machine that took him back to the silent movie days where he meets us as the Keystone Kops. Comedy gold. At least we didn't have to learn any crummy lines, but there was a lot of running round and round the Western saloon set (???) as Lenny cranked an old time camera and Terry bawled instructions through a megaphone from a director's chair. We had one rehearsal and then they let the audience in. The oldest person there was about ten.

Five minutes into the show we played our single, 'Sweet Schoolgirl'. Yeah, I know it doesn't stand the test of time, but it went down well with our nursery group. One bow and we had to dash to get into our Keystone clobber. Waiting to race back on I noticed two guys in modern day police uniforms standing behind one of the cameras.

The Beatles were on the show a week later, playing 'From Me to You' which went straight to number one in the Hit Parade. We didn't quite have the same affect on the viewing public. It certainly hadn't helped that we got our first national newspaper coverage with a photo of us in our Keystone Kops gear and the story of Clickettyclacks' Dudley being arrested on the set of Lenny the Lion's TV show for nicking the Birmingham Lord Mayor's wheels. 'Sweet Schoolgirl' was pulled from record shops across the UK and The Clickettyclacks disbanded for a while.

It was pre-Clickettyclacks time when Ernie Brown discovered us. Ernie ran the greengrocers on Bridge Road. That was the shop with the live goat who snuffled about the fruit and veg. counters. Very, very pre-Health & Safety. Ernie had been running the shop since the war and, bored with only a goat to speak to each day, he was looking to put some excitement into his life. Inspired by tales he'd heard in the press about the hit making 2i's Coffee Bar in London's Soho, he bought the knitwear shop next door and set about renovating it. His masterplan was to track down local talent to play there and hopefully join Tommy Steele and co. at the top of the pop charts. What could possibly go wrong? Well, Ernie was a gung-ho Christian for starters. Nothing wrong with that....in the right place, but birds and money were never high on Jesus's priorities. And birds and money were a huge part of why we got into the music business in the first place. The we at this point were The Ladders, me, Laurence, Richard and some bloke whose name I forget on bongos.

Ernie collared me one day as I was passing by. I'd been shopping round there since I was a tot. He spotted my guitar case and asked about the band. Before I left, he'd signed us up for the grand opening of the Go, Man, Go! Coffee Spot. That was still two months ahead but he promised he'd try getting us a few gigs in the meantime.

He came through pretty fast with the first gig a couple of nights later. It was at an old folks home in Ainsdale. It was the first time I'd been in such a place and I made my mind up that night that I'd never go in another no matter how long I lived. People reminisce fondly about the smell of the old Cavern Club but the Highfields Retirement Home had it beat hands down. It smelled of old people. Smelly old people. And that was just the bozos who ran the place. The décor was 1930's undertaker's parlour. The inhabitants had been arranged on high back chairs facing one end of the main living room where two standing lamps marked out our stage area. We could detect no sign of life in that audience other than the occasional trail of drool from an open mouth. I would guess that the average age was one hundred and twenty.

Ernie introduced us to a welcoming high-pitched fart from a woman in the front row. We kicked off with a Chuck Berry medley followed by a couple of Little Richard rockers. The silence when we came to the end was deafening, broken only by the crash of splintering glass from two picture frames we'd loosened from the wall. And then one of the undead spoke: 'Bloody rubbish this! What do they think we are? Kids?!' He had a fair point. We hadn't really put a set together taking into consideration our audience of stiffs. Hideous as the night was, I guess we learned something from it and Richard and I worked in a few speeded up numbers from the 1890's popular songbook for future gigs just in case. Actually, there were some great songs written back then once you electrify them.

I forget what our fee was for the Highfields gig but it certainly wasn't enough. You don't want to see that kind of thing when you are in your teens.

It was a week later Ernie got us a gig at his nephew's wedding. We feared the worst after the old folks horrors but this turned out to be a turning point in our thick heads. We actually went down a bundle. Every song took the roof off. It was a perfect audience as everyone was pissed off their heads. Ernie was the only one not to have a blast as he was concerned that the local vicar would cause a stink if he stuck his head inside the church hall and found his parishioners going loco to the jungle beats. The Ladders came away from the night knowing we had something going on. Now if we could just figure out what.

By cross-referencing our career with that other Liverpool band, I see that by sheer coincidence as members of the Beatles or Silver Beetles or Quarrymen, or whatever they were calling themselves at the time were painting the cellars of The Jacaranda for their new manager Alan Williams, The Ladders were painting the stage area of the Go, Man, Go Coffee Spot.

We'd gone Space Age for the décor, painting a moonscape with rising Earth and fiery rocket ship for the backdrop. Looked very effective in a Dan Dare, Pilot of the Future kind of way. The Grand Opening was at midday on a Saturday to guarantee maximum teenage customers. Ernie had even organised a ribbon cutting ceremony outside the shop doorway and booked Pinky & Perky, a well-known puppet act of the period to do the honours. It shows how celebrity starved we were at that point as their appearance caused quite a stir in the waiting crowd, despite their handler being in plain sight manipulating their strings. Many laughs and ooo's and aaahhhs as the two pigs pulled out a huge pair of scissors and cut the ribbon.

It was all looking good as we took to the stage with our instruments. It was like a mad January sale at the counter where the public were buying the American named beverages: Manhattan Milk Shake, Indiana Espresso, Colorado Coffee, and our own Corona fizz. Ernie took to the stage to announce us but to our horror, he brought on two priests from nearby Catholic churches.

'Before the boys get your feet tapping, Fathers Kelly and Kelly have kindly agreed to bless this new place of business and say a short prayer for the well-being and safe journey to the after-life for all our customers.'

As short prayers go, The Angelus simply doesn't cut it. By the third Hail Mary, I could see we were already losing members of our audience. And several more took to their heels when both priests pulled out their aspergillums and started sprinkling holy water in every direction. To top it off, the Kellys went round the remaining audience with collecting plates for their respective church roofs. On stage, we looked at each other and did the only thing that could possibly save the worsening situation. We played the Devil's music, crashing straight in with *Shakin' All Over*. It worked. The priests were out the door before the middle eight and the audience moved as one to get closer to the stage. Our legend was born that day. In our own heads admittedly, but we knew it was only a matter of time before the world would catch on. It was over five years as it turned out but that's showbiz for you. It's not the swiftest bird in the flock.

I thought I'd pulled at the end of our set as a starry-eyed girl called Angela bought me a Coke and offered to carry my guitar home. It turned out she'd got the biggest kick out of The Angelus and when the holy water hit her she said she felt like St Paul on the road to Damascus and it made her mind up to become a nun. Not quite what I was hoping for but it didn't spoil the overall high of the day.

TODAY

Ha! I've been invited back to my old school to give an *inspiring talk* to the students on this year's Prize Giving and Speech Day. This certainly proves that the school doesn't keep your reports and records on file. Will I do it? I don't know. It is the height of absurdity, so I just might. My memories of Speech Days of old were of some boring old duffer from the church or armed forces droning on and on as they attempted to encourage us to fight for Queen and country or Jesus. Maybe Richard and I should both go? I'm to RSVP to a guy who claims to be the school's Head of Marketing. Schools have marketing departments these days? Did I mention recently how much I hate everything? A school with a marketing department … words fail me. No they don't. What a load of utter bollocks. Well, I guess I've got to go and give my inspiring talk now. Those kids need me! Mr Marketing Manager might regret offering me the gig though.

Germany Calling has still taken occupation of my downstairs. Removal day deadline passed again with a single word of hope text from Orange: 'Soon, I promise'. Bloody agents, managers, Germans, musicians, parents, and bloody merchandise. Today we had a delivery of 200 boxes of every type of Bach Sisters merchandise. T-shirts, mugs, posters, pens, pyjamas, socks, underpants, ties, authorised hair dye, dog poop bags, cat litter trays, airplane sick bags, toilet rolls, and drain cleaner. It's like a mountain of hefty priced disposable crap just waiting in my main hall before moving out to clog up the world's oceans. Daddy and Mummy Bach are delighted with their branded goods and offer me a tote bag full of the shit.

'You like our new logo?' asks Mum.

'Brilliant,' I say, hoping she catches the tone.

Beaming Dad pulls on a hoodie featuring the girls throwing their guitars in the air. 'It represents the joy of their music. There are three hoodies to collect with each one showing the guitars getting higher in the air. The fans love collectability. The new album and this new merch will be the girls' breakthrough. They are my pension.'

No smile when he said this. Interesting to note Mum wasn't included in the pension plan. I almost felt sorry for the sisters except they are so bloody irritating so I didn't. Go, Dad, go, you miserable shrivelled get.

Speaking of irritating, Mina and Lena have got a new toy. It's a camera drone, which zips everywhere round the house taking high shots and chipping my finest chandeliers. They followed me with it as I took a walk to the chip shop today. I knew I should have kept that gun Elvis gave me back in 1969. Later, back home, I find the girls going through my old record collection. Laughing, they hold up my copy of ABBA's *Arrival* LP.

'Whose is this?' they ask accusingly.

'Mine.'

High screeches of disbelief.

'Wha-aatt? You can't actually like ABBA?! They are crap.'

I don't quite know what happened during the next twenty minutes but at the end of it the Bach family and their merchandise were scattered across my driveway waiting for a cab. You don't knock ABBA to me. I took delight in watching the unanswered messages, texts and emails mounting up from Orange over the rest of the day as the complete ABBA collection blasted out of the speakers around my house.

YESTERDAY

We started the Sixties dressed as Keystone Kops chasing a motheaten ventriloquist's dummy round a TV studio on a children's show. The dummy was famous. We weren't. But showbiz is nothing if not cruel and by 1969 Lenny the Lion was all but forgotten by a generation of kids preferring their puppets to have a touch more Supermarionation about them. As for us, we were at that legendary Toppermost of the Poppermost with the Beatles. Nobody expected us to get togged out in ridiculous costumes for kids' shows any more. We were now superstars and the public hung on every pronouncement we made from on high. And we were on high, baby! I think the TV stations must have been too as I was asked on to a programme called *Man of the Decade*. The idea behind the show was that John Lennon, Richard Burton and myself would come to the London Weekend TV studios and answer questions from a live audience. There would then be a telephone vote to determine which of us was the aforesaid Man of the Decade. A more stupid idea there has never been, but this was 1969 so we all three agreed to appear.

I remember spending an age trying to figure out what to wear. I had become very conscious of the fact that the psychedelic look of the last two years was out except for complete potheads and the general public who were finally being offered it by the main fashion houses. It was important to be setting trends rather than riding one from a couple of years ago. The show was being filmed on the fifth of November so in the end I got one of the band's designers to make me up a customised Guy Fawkes' outfit. The thigh-high boots set the satin cloak off nicely and the hat looked a lot better when I dispensed with the plume.

The ensemble looked a lot less fussy than some of the gear we'd worn over the previous few years so it was a bit irritating to arrive at the LWT Green Room and hear a familiar Scouse snort of derision.

'Penny for the Guy, mister!' Lennon, of course. Although I hadn't seen him since India, over a year ago, like everyone else on planet Earth I was aware of his current white-suited and heavy bearded look. He could have just stepped off the cover of *Abbey Road*.

'Alright, Jesus,' not my best comeback but as I was finding it difficult to unfasten the chain keeping the cloak in place round my neck at the time, it had to do. John was sprawled on a sofa facing the windows showcasing one of the best views up river to St Paul's and beyond. I thought he'd gained weight until Yoko uncurled herself from his arms and reached for a nearby pack of cigarettes and lighter.

'So Man of the Decade, eh?' I asked.

'Well that's very nice of you to admit it, Mike,' the Hard Day's Night smirk still in place behind the beard.

'Only the general public can decide that,' a booming voice hit the gods in every corner of the room. We turned and were duly dazzled by Hollywood at its most radiant. Not only Richard Burton but also Elizabeth Taylor. They actually shone and had the look as if they'd just stepped out of the nearest Playboy Club party. I've seen diamonds before and since but never as many or as big as those Liz was wearing that day. And yet somehow, she seemed to outshine the lot of them. If you could drag your eyes away from Liz, Dick was no slouch himself. He owned the room. For all their charisma, John and Yoko looked positively dingy by comparison. Guy Fawkes, on the other hand, held his own.

Eamonn Andrews was our host for the evening. Somehow I had managed to avoid his shows through the Sixties so this was our first meeting. Man, that guy could sweat up a storm. Even in the Green Room when he came in to say hi, his palm was a swamp. He and the director went over the running order with us – chat to each in turn, all together, and then throw it over to audience Q&A. Somehow this was going to make a three-hour programme. The Sixties was a different country.

I was on first and was happy to find they played our latest single, *Time & Space*, as I made the staircase entrance. Sounded good and a bunch of hippies in the audience got up and danced at the side of the set. Eamonn ran through my career from professional flop to global artist. I was impressed as I'd been too busy living it to look back until then. The laughs came in the right places despite Eamonn's best efforts to slow everything down to a crawl. It was like being interviewed by a well-meaning cow who was always three or four thoughts behind me. The sweat was now like a running tap.

The Lennons were on next as I moved up the sofa. They came down the staircase clutching a huge bucket of water between them to the accompaniment of *Give Peace a Chance*. With a heave, they placed the bucket on top of Eamonn's desk, leading to the inevitable first question, 'So what's with the bucket?' Actually, Eamonn ignored the bucket and asked something about John's original band The Quarrymen but I could see J&Y needed a stooge so I asked the question.

'I'm glad you asked, Michael,' said John. 'Yoko, would you like to explain the meaning of our bucket of water?'

'Yes, John, the water represents us all. Once upon a time we were all water before we took this form and things became mixed up. As water we were all one and one together. We flowed together. We swam together. We all thought in the same way and we were all happy.' This description went on for a lot longer until our first commercial break made Eamonn interrupt the utter gibberish. But John was not done yet. When the programme resumed, he lifted the bucket from the desk and poured it over the studio floor.

'You see how it flows everywhere? It goes over or round any obstacles with ease.'

'Yes,' agreed Yoko, 'to be as water is the way forward for the people across our planet. We must flow as one.'

Unfortunately, the camera crew were freaking out as one as the water sloshed around their feet and electricity sockets and the programme went to another commercial break while mops were brought in to prevent audience incineration.

We came back with Yoko playing bongos while screeching and John trying to look as if this was the most natural thing in the world. No mention was made of the Beatles through the whole interview but rather John and Yoko's peace campaign was the main talking point. I'm guessing Paul, George and Ringo couldn't give a shit.

'We could have world peace in a day if we just stopped listening to our so-called leaders and just counted the clouds in the sky,' said John in his rather belligerent way.

'Bollocks!' somebody shouted out from the audience, obviously a Rolling Stones fan.

'It's true,' cried Yoko. 'You just need to plant acorns and watch them grow.'

Eamonn tried to steer the conversation away from the volatile subject of peace to the avant garde area of Yoko's art. She spoke at length on this, and I don't believe anyone in the studio, including John, had a clue what she was going on about.

The Burtons were introduced and John and Yoko squeezed up beside me on the sofa. I don't know what she'd done while waiting to come and join us but I don't believe I've ever seen anyone or thing look as beautiful as Elizabeth Taylor did that night. It was quite breathtaking and it is unbelievable that she was the same woman who would hang out with that loon Michael Jackson a few decades later like some nightmare version of The Munsters.

Eamonn covered her life from *National Velvet* to *Cleopatra* before turning to Burton who disregarded the question about his origins and went into Welsh mode with a recitation from *Under Milk Wood*. Yoko looked a bit bemused until John whispered in her ear, 'It's good this.' And so it was, for the first two minutes, but by the time the next commercial break came round, ten minutes later, I think we all agreed that less is more with Dylan Thomas.

Next came questions from the audience. These ranged from the Vietnam war to the importance of fashion in music. I took the fashion query, leaving Vietnam to John and Yoko. Not surprisingly they were against and had an answer on how to end it with something called Dream Power. Liz and Dick were questioned on the difference between acting for stage and screen and whether they took their roles home with them. It was about this point that I noticed a disruption in the audience. The studio had been invaded by about thirty men dressed all in black and sporting dog collars. They looked to me like my old teachers, the Irish Christian Brothers. They came onto the set and sat down around us and on top of Eamonn's desk. Their leader or spokesperson announced to camera that this was a happening and that they were here to set the clock back one hundred years.

'We are Catholic Root and we are here to protest about real Catholicism being eroded to make it appealing to the perverted modern world.' He had a point, I suppose. Since 1961 the faith had been tinkered with in the hope of halting the rush for the exit brought about by the more enlightened times we were cruising through. I remember my Uncle Ged reacting in horror to news that the mass was going to be said in English rather than the standard Latin. 'Nobody'll understand a word.'

Catholic Root didn't even get a sentence out to the free world as we had already gone to another commercial break. By the time we came back, the merry band had been roughhoused out of the building by LWT security, pissed off at having let them sneak in in the first place.

I honestly can't remember just who became the Man of the Decade, but as I don't remember, I'm guessing it wasn't me. Liz should have walked it if you ask me.

TODAY

I'm up for the role of Doctor Who according to a full-page story in the *Daily Mirror*. They even have six quotes from me on how I intend to approach the part. I must be even more out of it than I thought as I could swear this is the first I've heard about it. Apparently I can't wait to get to grips with the Daleks and I'm considering playing the Doctor as a trans gender.

In equally disturbing news, the Bach Sisters have been signed to perform on the LIDL supermarket TV Christmas advert.

Orange rings. Tour coming together well. No details yet. I'm fast reaching the couldn't care less mood. I've always got Doctor Who to fall back on. As always with Orange, there is BIG NEWS coming.

The BIG NEWS coming comes earlier than expected when I find Orange banging on my door later in the day.

'Prepare to love me even more than you already do, if that's possible, luv!' she waltzes into the kitchen and rattles the tea cups and pot. Over tea and biscuits she informs me that she sold the idea of a Dream Daffodils theatrical musical to Vincent at BINK Publishing. He's going to fund the whole thing and put the show on in the West End before a move to Broadway.

'We're just trying to find a suitable writer to create a storyline we can drop your finest songs onto,' Orange explained. 'We want somebody hip and cool like Ben Elton was thirty years ago. You guys can just sit back and watch the money come in.'

'Well we might want more input than that,' I quibbled. 'We don't want some crappy storyline like the ABBA and Queen things.'

We agreed to meet with Richard later in the week and talk through the best way forward. I have no problem with sitting back and watching money come in but I don't want us to link our best music to some utter tosh cobbled together by a flavour of the month comedy writer.

YESTERDAY

Elvis got us, of course, from the first time we heard him on the family wireless. As I bring it to mind, I can actually smell the moment and see us all sitting round the dinner table. I can smell the lamb, the mint sauce, the coal fire, but most of all, Elvis. He lived up to all expectations when I saw him for the first time a year later on Richard's family TV. I certainly questioned my sexuality that day.

So, can you picture the scene and feel the moment nearly ten years later in 1966 as those chart topping Dream Daffodils head over to meet the King of Rock & Roll on the set of his latest movie, *Paradise, Hawaiian Style*. We weren't in Hawaii but on the Paramount back lot in Hollywood. Hey, that'd do for us Liverpool boys. I just remember heading into the studio, which was decked out with palm trees and lagoons and about a thousand Playboy models in skimpy (for the period) bikinis. Elvis was on set rehearsing a song with a little girl. I see from my LP soundtrack that the number must have been *Queenie Wahine's Papaya*, not one of his greatest hits. Other songs include, *Scratch My Back, A Dog's Life, House of Sand,* and *Drums of the Islands.* Yeah, the Pelvis was a long way from *Heartbreak Hotel.* But we didn't care. It was Elvis fucking Presley for God's sake!

He even came over and spoke to us. I mean, I know we were big at that time but Elvis was something else. We found it weird that he would even notice us. I'm not saying we were humble. We were never that but Elvis is kind of like Mickey Mouse or King Arthur. A legend. Maybe even a myth so it was hard to take in that we were standing in the same spot on the same planet at the same time period. And the really strange thing was that despite the crappy songs he was singing for the movie, he looked and talked like Elvis.

I asked him what the movie was about.

'Paradise, Hawaiin style,' he laughed. 'That about sums it up. Oh, add helicopters, dogs and lots of girls. What more do you want in a movie?'

'Sounds a lot better than Zulu,' I joked, and he laughed. Elvis laughed at my dumb joke. I made Elvis laugh. He then introduced us to his co-star, Suzanna Leigh, and I don't remember noticing Elvis again for the rest of our time at the studio. Suzanna is another story though.

TODAY

Richard and I turn up to discuss the musical with Orange and bump into the Bach Sisters and family just exiting Ye Olde Cheshire Cheese pub on Fleet Street. They hug me, for God's sake! And the smiles!! We head downstairs and find Orange in her usual spot. She's sitting in deep conversation with a spotty Herbert I recognise from somewhere. As we approach she looks up and rummages in her bag before pulling out a bundle of papers to wave triumphantly in my face.

'The tour is in place, luvs. Get these dates in your diaries and calendars and get rehearsing!'

As I get out my specs to read through the dates, Orange grabs the pages from me and hurries on.

'Never mind the tour right now. This is Dave Locke, the comedian's comedian. He's going to write your musical.'

I looked at Richard and we both turned as one to Orange with the rhetorical question: 'Is he?!'

Now I recognised his face from clicking past it ten thousand times over the last year in the search for decent TV. BBC comedy darling of the moment. Stand up and his own chat show where guests go on to be his stooge. The spotlight never falters from Dave. In my ever-growing list of things I hate, Dave Locke is round about number 55 with a bullet. Richard and I had watched a whole show of his once and taken it in turns to come up with more disgusting swear words each time his face was on screen. You could say we didn't take to him. So Dave had quite a sales job ahead of him if he was hoping to link his name to ours.

'I just want to say I'm a big fan of the Daffodils and always have been,' Dave stood up to shake our hands. Richard and I actually laughed out loud at this.

'Congrats, Dave,' said Richard. 'That's the first time you've made us laugh.' Give him his due, that made Dave laugh, and he headed off to get us drinks.

'Behave, boys,' said Orange. 'He's got a fabulous idea for the musical. It's exactly the kind of thing that works today. It'll run for years in every major city across the world.'

Dave returns and asks us a dozen questions from all periods of our career. He is most certainly Nerd Supreme Fan. He looks at us the way I remember looking at Elvis.

'Right, well, the idea I have for the musical is pretty simple. The other night I sat and listened to every single and every album you've ever made.'

'You should see a doctor about that,' said Richard.

'The idea for the musical was already there in your songs,' Dave continued, not missing a beat. 'Your songs are about love, passion, hurt, compassion, all the feelings we all go through in life. And so we tell the story of mankind as we follow one family from cavemen to the Space Age and show how even for our technological wonders, we still share the same feelings as our ancestors.'

Richard and I turned to look at each other and I could see the 'bollocks' comment forming on his lips when Dave went on:

'And the whole show would be performed in the nude as we want to strip away all pretensions from our cast.'

'Nude?' Richard and I both said the word in harmony. Well, that changed everything.

YESTERDAY

Nudity had changed everything for us once before back in 1964. We were going under the name The Heroes and we were worried that life was passing us by. After a few false bites from London based agents and managers during 1963, we were still stuck in Liverpool as The Beatles and various other local groups took off in what became known as The British Invasion of the US. It was all headline news in the Liverpool Echo, Crosby Herald and even the national papers. Every word we read stuck in our collective throat. We knew how good we were by this time and had a considerable following across the region but we were ready to forget our roots and go global. By June The Beatles had conquered the planet and were about to launch their third LP and first movie. A movie!!! We were still scrabbling round to get enough cash to take our birds to the movies never mind starring in one.

Richard and I met at the Kardomah for lunch one day and we were both equally miserable. We knew something had to happen and fast or we'd end up as the Liverpool band who should have made it but didn't.

'We need a gimmick,' I said.

'Fuck off!' replied Richard. 'No gimmicks! We've always said that.'

It's true, we had. Early on back in the Fifties there had been a flurry of bands with gimmicks like midget harmonica players or a female drummer. We'd always thought things like that were crap because, well, because they were. But here we were in the Sixties and nothing was happening.

'How long do you want to go on getting nowhere?' I asked. 'This whole scene has been a drag since the Fabs cracked the US and we're still playing the bloody Jive Hive in Crosby.'

'This is true,' agreed Richard. 'I'm thinking of getting out. My uncle's offered me a job in the toy department at Lewis's.'

'You're joking?'

'No joke. Regular pay. No ups and downs hoping we're going to make it big one day. And you know, we're going to be a joke soon. The guys who were left behind.'

'Fuck Lewis's!' I insisted. 'We're going to make it. We're going to blow The Beatles off the front pages. We're going to do something so big that we'll be the only band everyone's talking about for the next month.' I was pretty passionate. I certainly slammed the tabletop a couple of times and I remember one of our cheeseburgers leapt in the air and hit the floor. Richard was shaken out of his blue funk. He smiled and asked, 'One question. How?'

Indeed, that was the question. It had always been the question since the day we met but now was the time to headbutt it out of the stadium.

The stadium in this case turned out to be the Jive Hive in Crosby. That's what we called it, mainly cos that sounded a lot better than its real name of St Luke's Church Hall. It was two days later and, despite my passion over the cheeseburgers, I'd still not come up with any idea likely to get us noticed. It was a Saturday afternoon and it was a pretty feeble turnout, with something like thirty people making up the audience. Most of these were our own dedicated following; slightly deranged with eyes that would stare long after polite society would look away. The boys and I used to joke that we could get them to do anything for us, and Laurence, if hard up on a Saturday night, would often prove that point.

This came to mind as we were in the middle of our third number, *Beautiful Dreamer,* and I realised that we were giving about 20% our normal full-steam ahead. I knew this was generated by the band's subconscious as we headed down to rock bottom before the inevitable break-up. All the frustrations of the last months came to a head as the song droned to its end and I turned on the band.

'Fucking wake up, you cunts!' I bawled. Instantly recognising that this wouldn't exactly help the general mood and attitude I turned to the audience and shouted out an idea that came from I know not where, your honour. And that's my defence, and I rest by it to this day.

'EVERYBODY TAKE OFF YOUR CLOTHES AND DANCE NOW!'

Nutty Tina and Weirdo Wendy up front had their tops off before I'd even got to the end of the sentence. The rest of the audience stared in disbelief until we rocked into *Kansas City* and all but two of them followed suit. We had an audience of guys and girls stark bollock naked jiving in front of us. I looked round at the boys. My slight critique was forgotten as they beamed and blasted out the song as never before. I don't think we've ever sounded as good since that moment in Crosby's Jive Hive. We peaked.

Of course, we were also banned from playing the Jive Hive ever again. Luckily, someone had taken photos during that final performance and somehow they ended up on the newsdesk of the *News of the World*, Britain's scummiest and consequently most popular Sunday newspaper. Things took off swiftly after that. We were denounced in parliament and church pulpits across the country. I highly recommend it to anyone wanting to break into the music business. Within two weeks we had a 80 date tour of slightly dodgy venues up and down the UK. And then the call came from Decca and Pye. We were booked to audition for a record contract with both companies. The band had lost their latest manager about three months earlier when we'd accidently got his car stuck in the quicksand down near Crosby beach, so we were representing ourselves. Richard and I played off Pye and Decca against each other. We had a great feeling of nothing to lose so just acted on instinct, much as we had when we'd lost the car in the quicksand, but this time things worked out.

TODAY

Email from BINK Publishing: Hi Mike, I'm cc'ing in Vicki Mann, who is taking over the edits on your book. Mike, Vicki. Vicki, Mike. Vincent.

Vicki Mann: Thanks, Vincent. Hi Mike!

Mike Simon: Vincent, what happened to Gloria?

BINK Publishing: She's gone on maternity leave. You'll love Vicki. She's really into your scene. Loves the whole Dream Daffodils catalogue.

Mike Simon: It says in the Sun that Gloria Benton is suing BINK over sex allegations. Isn't that my Gloria?

BINK Publishing: No, no, no. That's just tabloid garbage. We're suing the Sun over the story.

Vicki Mann: Hi Vincent, Who are the Dream Daffodils?

Mike Simon: Vicki, was I supposed to get this?

Vincent sent some idiot to the house this afternoon to talk marketing for the book. I don't know what planet marketing people come from but can we please bomb it now? They were called Daisy and Trey and were as annoying as their names. They laughed a lot, no matter what I said. I'm sure I probably said a few funny things over the tea but they had the same delayed reaction each time before they would guffaw. I know that this means one of two things. 1. They didn't get the joke in the first place and were being polite. 2. They got the joke, didn't find it funny, and were simply sucking up.

They spoke in that god-awful lingo of the marketing world, which makes me want to strangle puppies. Apparently Vincent has okayed Advertising Elasticity on all stages of the product (my book) and he is currently Affiliate Networking to make sure we choose the right Brand Identity and Card Rate. There's going to be substantial Direct Marketing including Direct Response, Counter Advertising and Deceptive Advertising. They look forward to a Galvanometer Test and a Focus Group Interview as soon as they have a few more pages. The Gross Audience is undecided at this moment. No word yet on Horizontal Discount or Holding Power of the product. They are keeping their eyes on the Key Success Factors and Leave Behind. Their main objectives over the next few months will include Penetrated Market Analysis, Product Life Cycle, Product Placement and the Referral Premium. Our USP is, of course, our Target Audience.

Having lost track after the first biscuit, I nodded along and escorted them off the premises directly after they paused to take breath. It's strange. I see these people for what they are … non-entities, but still they leave me in a seething rage that we share the same planet and that they are employed. I've no idea why I let them get to me in such a way. Must be something in my make-up. Thanks, Mum and Dad. I head upstairs, pull the old punching bag from a cupboard and beat the crap out of it for the rest of the afternoon.

YESTERDAY

Paul McCartney's 21st birthday was a hoot, but only in retrospect from fifty years on. At the time, the day itself was a bloody nightmare. It didn't start off that way. We all felt that day in June 1963 was going to be a turning point for us. And so it was, putting us back to square one for the umpteenth time. 1963 was a hot year with Liverpool acts topping the charts just about every week. The Beatles led the way, followed by anyone else their manager Brian Epstein signed up. We'd known for about a year that Epstein and his NEMS organisation were the only sure way to get us up and out of Merseyside. We'd invited him to every gig we had but with no luck. Fair dues to the guy, he'd been pretty busy with the other acts and his record department in Whitechapel.

We really thought our luck had changed when Laurence bounded into the dressing room before a gig at the Iron Door early in June and told us we might want to fall down at his feet and praise him.

'Get down, lads, we've cracked it. I was in the Gents opposite Waterloo train station earlier today and who should walk in? Brian bloody Epstein, that's who! Well, we got talking and one thing led to another and the upshot is he wants to see us and he's invited us to play at McCartney's 21st birthday in a couple of weeks.'

As unlikely as this sounded, Laurence showed us a note scribbled on NEMS stationery giving us entry to Paul's party at his Aunty Gin's on the 18th. And there was the Epstein signature. We played well that night at the Iron Door. I remember thinking we'd have to change the location of the place Laurence met Eppy as we didn't want our legend starting in a local gent's bog.

Speaking of legends, McCartney's 21st birthday party has gone down in the books as the day The Beatles got their first national press thanks to a drunken John Lennon beating up Bob Wooler, the compere from the Cavern. Well, NEMS had to give the newspapers some kind of story because they certainly didn't want them getting hold of the full facts of what went down that day and night at Aunty Gin's. We turned up early, so early in fact that only Aunty Gin was there. She was typical Liverpool and not fazed by us or the amps, guitars and drums and simply turned us out into the back yard to set up while she put the kettle on. We'd decided to pull out all the stops to impress Epstein and had pooled every penny we had to get suited and booted. We'd heard this was the first thing he did for each signing so we wanted to seem keen. Cool suits actually in different colours to differentiate between us. Wouldn't work on black and white telly but should do for Aunty Gin's back garden.

Brian looked a little off when he arrived. He had a black eye for one thing and a jagged rip in his immaculate overcoat. He disappeared into a back room with Aunty Gin for half an hour and we could hear what seemed to be heavy sobbing. When he came back out, he was the Brian we'd grown used to seeing in a million interviews. Smooth and relaxed. It looked like Aunty Gin had been at him with her make-up to practically conceal his black eye. He seemed happy to see us but we were a bit thrown when he told us, 'Those suits will have to go. They're hideous. But don't worry, I thought ahead and have something for you out in the car.'

He returned after a few minutes with several shopping bags, which he handed to each of us. Inside we found leather jackets and trousers. Expensive stuff but a bit bewildering as we all knew the first thing he'd done with The Beatles was to get them out of leathers.

'You boys have the right look for leather outfits,' he explained. 'The Beatles just looked as if they were playacting.' It was a compliment of sorts, I suppose, and if Brian Epstein thought we suited leathers then we'd wear leathers. At that stage we would have happily worn ballerina tutus if he'd said it would make the difference.

We had to laugh on pulling on the kecks and jackets to find that they came complete with the legendary twat hats. And that's what really kicked off the bigger problem of the day. It's impossible not to ponce around if you are dressed completely in leather and wearing those well-named flat hats. That's exactly what we were doing when Lennon walked in on us. I think he heard Richard's fruity comment, 'Look at us, we're early Beatles off for a stroll down the Reeperbahn, looking for trade.'

On a normal day, John would have probably let it pass, but from the state of him I'd say he'd been celebrating Paul's birthday for the last week. He waded in and knocked said twat hat off Richard's head, somehow causing them both to tumble over one of Aunt Gin's wotnots with a splintering crash. Lots of fucks and cunts and shitheads ensued as the two of them wrestled around the parlour floor. I still laugh when I remember Richard's return volley to John's gutter tongue lashing: 'Push off, tie-boy!' You can take the boy out of Blundellsands but you can't take the Blundellsands out of the boy. His mother would have been proud at such restraint. It was at this moment that Bob Wooler entered the room and roared with laughter at seeing the boys tangled together on the floor.

'I always knew you were one of us, Lennon,' he cackled. And then, just in case John hadn't heard it over the scuffle, he said it again.

'I always knew you were a great poof, John!'

John certainly heard this. From the look on his face, we all knew that murder was about to be done. We did the decent thing and cleared a path for him to reach Bob rather than taking out his wrath on one of us. And no doubt murder would have been done if Lennon hadn't brought up his breakfast and last night's dinner at that precise moment. Aunty Gin entered the room, surveyed the sawdust of her wotnot, the bucketload of puke and Lennon, and now it seemed likely we were going to be witness to a double murder at Paul's 21st birthday party.

'You great lummox, Lennon!' bawled Aunty Gin. 'That wotnot's been in the family since Great Uncle Gerard brought it home from France in 1918. He might as well of saved himself the bother.' This was said with such venom that John looked quite sheepish as he wiped the puke from his mouth. He was sent to the back yard to fetch in a shovel and bucket and set to work cleaning up the parlour. We probably made the mistake of nudging each other and tittering at his labours.

'Hey, John, you missed a bit!' kind of thing. Bob Wooler didn't help as he kept coming back in and making comments such as, 'You'll make someone a lovely wife one day, John!'

We were pulled away from this entertainment by Laurence who spotted two of The Shadows outside the parlour window, turning up for the party. It was Bruce and Hank, unmistakeable having enjoyed the last five years on our telly screens and at the top of the charts with Cliff. We let them in at the front door and attempted to not seem impressed, which wasn't easy as we all were mightily impressed. The Shadows were about as professional as you could ever get in showbiz. To be honest, we never achieved their air of professionalism even at our height. Yes, we conquered the US and they didn't, but they were the pros. Apart from Epstein, the rest of the partygoers looked a right bunch of tattyheads by comparison to Hank and Bruce. They stood politely to one side in the kitchen and viewed everyone else like you do through viewing windows at a zoo. This was the Liverpool Life enclosure.

Throughout the afternoon more of the extended McCartney family turned up along with Ringo, Paul and George. We knew Ringo a little bit from his Rory Storm Hurricaning days. In fact we were the wise guys at the back of the crowd at the Cavern Club shouting 'We want Pete!' on that early *Some Other Guy* film clip. In other words, we knew him well enough to have a laugh with. So we couldn't resist telling him about the incident with John. He laughed, I think. It was always difficult to know if Ringo found something funny or not as his natural expression was bored going on gloomy. I always thought the natural role for him when he kicked off his film career was to play Eeyore.

'Thank goodness we got the moptop cut instead of the twat hats,' he said, flooding his Coke with a whisky. 'I wouldn't have joined the band if they'd still been wearing those.'

I don't think John was having any of the Coke in his whisky that afternoon. He staggered from one room to the other, looking more pissed and pissed off with each passing hour. Round about 3pm we headed out to the back yard, plugged in and played a near perfect version of *Happy Birthday To You* for the man of the hour. Paul looked suitably embarrassed while George and Ringo took delight in joining in for the *dear Paulie* line. Duty done, we kicked straight into a hard rocking *Great Balls of Fire* and it was great to see Hank and Bruce nodding along appreciatively. By our fifth number I noticed that Brian was standing at the back of the crowd with a happy smile on his face. I looked over at Richard and Laurence and we knew we'd cracked the Big Time. Unfortunately opportunity stopped knocking directly after that song when a drunken snarl was heard from somewhere in the crowd.

'Fucking rubbish this! They play like kids!' For one horrible moment I had a flashback to our gig long ago at the old folk's home. It wasn't the old coot though, who was surely long in his grave by now, it was, of course, John Winston Lennon. I saw Brian head over to attempt to sort him out as we went into the next number. John wasn't for sorting though and kept up a steady stream of heckling through and in between each song, his golden tones heard even above our amps.

At least half of our crowd peeled off to head inside to get away from the on-going uproar. John sat himself down at a garden table with a plate of party food in front of him. Every so often he would lob a sandwich or sausage on a stick at one of us as we ignored the bastard and carried on. At the end of our set John gave us the slow handclap and shouted across to Brian, 'There's no way you're signing those losers. Sign them and we're gone.' Epstein ignored the remark and headed back inside.

'I'll fucking kill the dickhead!' snarled Laurence as we packed up our kit. 'There's no way Epstein's going to sign us with fatgob bellyaching about us.' It seemed pretty unlikely that Brian would choose us over The Sensation of the Universe. However, Brian came back out and invited us inside to get a bit of birthday cake. Lennon seemed to have disappeared and there was the usual joking and singing and high party spirits going down inside. After a while, Laurence came up to me and asked if he could borrow my camera. It was a good camera, flash and everything. I didn't really like other people using it so I asked him what he needed it for. He told me to come upstairs in five minutes and enter the back bedroom snapping as I came. I assumed he had some bird he wanted to get porno pix of so I was up for that.

Except, it wasn't some bird. It was an unconscious Lennon across the bed with his kecks round his ankles and Laurence in, shall we say, a compromising position. The flashing camera roused the blotto Beatle and he took in the situation in a, well, a flash. It had a remarkably sobering effect on him. He was off the bed and pulling up his pants with one hand while he grabbed a table lamp with the other and charged at us. Laurence and I tumbled over each other as we headed downstairs, my main concern being to keep my camera from harm. John roared like a freight train as he chased us round and round the back yard. Somehow a shovel, a pickaxe, a garden gnome and Bob Wooler got involved in the fracas. It ended when John almost garrotted himself on Aunty Gin's washing line. It was at that moment that the guy from the Daily Mirror walked in the back gate.

Needless to say, Brian Epstein never signed us, but I do have in a bank vault a set of remarkable photos of John Lennon that I have always known will be my pension if this music business thing doesn't work out.

TODAY

Down the Cheshire Cheese to meet Agent Orange after a series of ever more excited texts, emails and phone messages, all ending with the invitation to 'come and meet the future. Your future!' Drinks were already in as she patted the seat for me to join her.

'What has been the biggest problem facing The Dream Daffodils in recent years?' she asked.

'Dementia? Arthritis? False teeth? Flatulence?'

'Pfff! Don't be silly. It's your audience dying off. Nobody's getting any younger and your original audience has been dropping like flies over the last couple of years.'

'Well, thank you for that greeting.'

'Shush and listen. I've solved the problem. We need to turn the next generation onto the Daffodils.'

'Yeah, good luck with that, Orange. There are few things teenagers rave about more than old crips in their eighties.'

'Exactly,' agreed Orange. 'So we need to be sneaky and introduce them to your music through one of their own. That's why I've got a hip new band recording an album of your greatest hits to zap the kids with. We'll launch the album and your book just before the tour and bingo, you'll get a Twenty-First century audience to revitalise all things Daff.'

Lacking in taste as the idea was, I could see it made sense. As far back as the Sixties The Beatles had introduced a new audience to the works of Little Richard and Chuck Berry.

'So who's the band?' I asked. As if on cue, the Bach Sisters and their parents walked across the bar to join us.

Hugs all round, of course. Stupid bleeding beaming faces. Dad proudly carrying a sack over his shoulder, which he empties across our table.

57

'Our latest merchandise. We would love you to have it for all you are doing for us.' Mouse pads, stickers, baseball caps, rulers, pencils, a duvet cover and pillow-cases, all emblazoned with images of the girls with doglike ear to ear smiles.

'You are looking very groovy, Mike,' says Mila.

'Far out, man!' agreed Lena.

I could feel my gorge rising.

'Let me stop you there, girls. I was groovy for one brief moment back in 1967 but luckily saw what a twat I looked in the mirror and quickly rectified it.'

The stupid smiles continued although I could see in the eyes that they couldn't follow my reasoning. I noticed that they had swapped their normal Pound Shop Bavarian fashions for expensive Sixties Flower Power period recreations. Mila even had a daisy tattooed on her left cheek.

'It's been a blast recording some of your hot numbers from way back. We really dig them, don't we, Lena?'

'You cats were the best,' Lena nodded.

I had to put a stop to this desecration of English/American slang.

'There's only one person who could ever get away with using the word cats to describe people. And Keith isn't here today so please cut it out.' Inevitable uncomprehending smiles all round although I think I may have glimpsed a slight 'I'll kill you, you bastard' look from Mila, deep behind her eyes. Dad then leant over and pressed play so I could watch the brand new video they had just completed to accompany the single off the album. It was our biggest hit from September 1967, *My Rainbow*, with its two minutes of song and four minutes of chant. All this a whole year before *Hey Jude* was released! The Bach Sisters' version was infuriatingly perfect. Germanically perfect, leaving heart and soul on the studio floor. Or is that review just me with my new found racism towards the Bachs?

'It would make sense to get you on *This Morning* raving about the sisters, Mike,' said Orange.

'Not gonna happen,' I answered after splattering her with a mouthful of *Olde Museum*. '

'A quote will do. Leave that to me.'

'No bloody quotes either!' I banged down my pint soaking the scattered merchandise. 'Let them do what we had to do. Get there on their own merits or not at all.' Bloody hell, I was starting to sound like my Grandfather. Maybe my Great Grandfather. Orange did her best agent/manager bit for them, arguing back and forth with my blunt refusals to do anything to support their career. In the end even she could see my mood was in for the duration and so called a cheery end to the meeting saying she had plenty of other ideas that would kickstart the album. I would happily kickstart both the album and artiste into the nearest skip. I honestly don't know where this anger has come from but it would seem I'm not letting go of it.

YESTERDAY

It was Autumn 1964 when our assault on the Hit Parade started in earnest. It had taken us exactly two years longer than The Beatles but we were finally there. The record that did it was *Naked Love* on the Pye label. We were encouraged to play up to our naughty image as created in the pages of the *News of the World*. Mildly raunchy by today's standards, the 45rpm was duly banned by the BBC, which immediately gave it a cool status it really didn't deserve. Pirate Radio picked up on it and it sailed merrily to the Toppermost of the Poppermost, knocking the Dave Clark Five back to Tottenham. Questions were raised in both parliament and pulpit and various children were expelled from schools up and down the country for bringing the record into the classroom. We really couldn't have asked for a better launch. Bumping into Mick Jagger down the *Bag of Nails* club one night we got him to give us a fantastic quote which we passed onto the press: 'Brian likes the record but Keith and I think it's a bit rude. We wouldn't let any kids of ours go and see The Heroes. I mean, you don't know quite what might happen with those guys.' That was it. We'd arrived.

Our first proper full UK tour kicked off back in Liverpool early in November. We weren't playing the little clubs this time but filling the Empire Theatre. Topping the bill, of course, which was filled with a strange selection of stars from the US including Kookie from *77 Sunset Strip*, Adam from *Bonanza*, the kid from *The Rifleman*, and the Singing Nun. We played 78 dates up and down the country, which was a fair slog but we were on a high with things finally going our way. Most theatre managements put out a warning in the foyer that nudity of any kind wouldn't be tolerated during the performance. This didn't stop many members of each audience whipping off their clothes during our final number. I was pleased to see the Singing Nun watching from the wings and chuckling to herself. She got showbiz and didn't equate it with being a pathway to damnation. I remember that she always seemed to enjoy getting quite merry at each after show party and on the tour bus between gigs. The Americans enjoyed the British excess too, shaking their heads in wonder at each new outrage along the way and the fact that nobody enjoyed it more than our travelling companion the Singing Nun. I think most Americans think the British are quite loopy but they are won over by the charm of our cobbles and accents.

TODAY

I have a new fan. When I woke up this morning, there she was lying in bed next to me. I was not on the piss last night so I knew at once that this was not someone I had invited into my home. There are few things more startling that waking to find eyes like hers staring at you. She had that look we all recognise in the business of a fan who has stepped over the line into the world of fanatic. I knew instantly that I was her religion. It has been many years since I've leapt out of bed in quite so sprightly a manner. She instantly had the phone out and was taking selfies with my bare arse and bollocks in the background. God knows where they will end up. Hopefully enlarged to poster size wherever they are. I hit the panic button as I pulled on my kecks. First time I'd had to use it since its installation back in December 1980. Despite austerity cutbacks, the police were round pretty sharpish but not before my madwoman had asked me to sign six copies of her favourite solo LP of mine, *Blazing* from 1972. She told me her name was Raven and stood there while I signed, quite oblivious to the fact that she was naked. I couldn't see any sign of her clothes in my bedroom so I must assume she arrived that way.

The police let themselves in and raced up the stairs calling out my name. Raven panicked at the commotion and ran over to try and open the window for a deadly getaway. She'd be lucky. Those windows haven't opened since I had the house painted by the cowboy decorator two years ago. A policewoman coaxed her down from the windowsill and wrapped a blanket from the bed round her. I gave her the signed LPs as she was escorted away and she thanked me and said the thing I least wanted to hear:

'I'll see you soon.' I swear she hadn't blinked once during our whole encounter.

I spent the afternoon and evening with Richard and Dave Locke going over ideas for the musical. The first few hours Richard and I spent nixing anything Dave suggested, just for fun. The rest of the time we'd come up with the very same suggestions, act as if it was the first time we'd heard the idea and rave about them:

'That's the kind of thing you should be coming up with, Dave.'

Returning home after midnight I saw the glow before I saw the fire engines. Pulling into my drive was like arriving in Hell. Firemen and hoses racing everywhere, in shadow play against the roaring flames, which seemed to touch the sky. I could barely see the house for the blinding fire. Even the trees in the garden were blazing away.

And speaking of *Blazing*, that was the word the police found painted on the garden wall much later that morning.

YESTERDAY

Looking back, it's hard to pinpoint the worst moments of our slow, and I mean tediously tortoiselike slow rise to stardom, simply because there were so many make-you-want-to-give-up dreary times along the way. Even after we 'made it', the money still took a while to come through. One moment that I've tried to block out of all memory banks occurred in 1965 thanks to yet another in our endless line of would-be managers. I can't even remember this guy's name but he owned a fish and chip shop in St John's Road in Liverpool's Waterloo, so at least we were well fed during his reign. In my hand I have a flyer for that one tour he masterminded. It's a typical arty early Sixties look to the design. Lightning bolts flash engagingly round the title of the tour: SHOW OF SHOWS! A Music Hall line-up of acts leap off the page thanks to a surplus of exclamation marks: COMPERE JOE SYKES! MAGICAL MARVEL THE GREAT SHAMIR! 100 XYLOPHONES WITH BERT & TAMI! US!!!! GOD'S SINGING NUN! THE GPO's SINGING POSTMAN! Yes, that was the bill. As they say, you wouldn't get away with it today. A package tour from Hell for us. We were stuck on a coach and in hotels and venues with that bunch for three solid weeks slogging backwards and forwards across the UK. The Singing Nun and the Singing Postman were the main problem. They absolutely hated each other. Both their careers were already on the downward turn by this time and the realisation of being one-hit wonders was obviously hard to swallow for them both. Also, the Singing Nun believed that the Singing Postman had stolen her act of being a singer from an unlikely profession. We'd toured with the nun six months before when she was full of all the joys of life, but six months is a long time in showbiz, even for a nun, or maybe especially for a nun. After each show, back at the hotel, she would hit the communion wine in the bar and end up staggering through the halls and landings bawling abuse in Latin at the Singing Postman. I don't think she realised we had done Latin during our school years and so we happily translated the worst for the Postie. I remember there were a lot of cocksuckers and mothersuperiorfuckers in her rants. I guess we may have mistranslated as we had never really mastered the language. For the last show of the tour, both nun and postman were determined to out-do the other. To that end they both brought on mass choirs of nuns and postmen to back them on their greatest hit. I have a memory of standing in the wings with Richard and Laurence, surrounded by angry nuns as we watched 100 postmen on stage belting out 'Have You Got a Light, Boy?' Richard turned to me and gloomily remarked, 'Rock and Roll is dead!'

YESTERDAY

In May 1966 we made what would be our one and only released film. Thank goodness for that. I mean, what a strange time we grew up in when pop stars would immediately be signed up to act in a movie. Act! Us!! And you were given no lessons or helpful tips, just a script and a shout of 'ACTION!' There really were some stinkers made by various groups and singers in the early to mid Sixties. Freddie and the Dreamers, Gerry and the Pacemakers, Cliff, Heinz, the Dave Clark Five, and Elvis, of course. Most of them were variations on the Forties Judy Garland and Mickey Rooney 'We'll do the show here!' type of story. At least ours wasn't one of those. It was called *Out of Time*, and the storyline, which we came up with ourselves, had us being transported back to the days of the Wild West and attempting to see if we could make a Rock and Roll tour work in those pre electricity days as we hit Tombstone, Dodge City, and the Ponderosa. This final stop was thanks to our connection with Pernell Roberts who played Adam Cartwright on TV's *Bonanza*. Richard, Laurence and I all fancied playing cowboys and we were on such a high now the hits were finally coming that we thought acting would be a doddle. It wasn't as anyone who has seen the film would agree. We had meant to play it completely straight but after seeing the first day's rushes we and the producers recognised that the only way forward was to pile on the ham and play it for out and out laughs. Well, it makes me laugh if I see clips today. As actors we are all hopeless and it doesn't help that we have professional actors around us. It just makes us look even worse. It probably helped the real actors when they had to play the cowfolk being amazed by these strange creatures from the future. It didn't take much acting talent to stare in bewilderment at us. Speaking of cowboys, Buck Owens once

66

said, 'All you've got to do is act naturally', but he never told us how. Thank goodness for the songs. We had ten of those in the film and at least six of them still stand up.

The love interest was played by Brigitte Bardot with whom Richard, Laurence and I had been deeply in lust since our schooldays. Meeting her in the flesh didn't help abate our schoolboy passion. She looked exactly like the Brigitte we'd poured over, literally, in the fan mags of the Fifties. Even better actually as this one was breathing, and boy did she breathe. Whenever she spoke to you she would stand toe-to-toe and lean in so that you would feel every breath. I think this was because she was very short-sighted but none of us were complaining. I remember that she smoked a lot more than us, which is really saying something. She was like a chimney, immediately lighting up directly after each scene and always lighting the next fag from the last.

Aficionados of Sixties pop movies will be aware that each film would usually bung in a comedian or comedy actor to help keep the viewers happy. Even the Fabs had old man Steptoe, Wilfred Brambell, Roy Kinnear and Victor Spinetti, although apparently they ended up cutting Frankie Howard out of *Help* for some reason. We thought long and hard about who we wanted in our movie after Brigitte. To this day I think we chose well by bringing in Charlie Cairoli and company direct from Blackpool Tower Circus. Charlie was probably the most famous clown in the world at that point in time, and quite rightly. I'd seen him live when I was taken to the circus as a treat on my eighth birthday and was blown away with his highly subversive *Chaos in the Classroom* sketch involving a huge saw and hammer, and about 300 gallons of water. The company he brought along to our film were little Jimmy Buchanan and white-faced Paul. Charlie and Paul were master musicians on trumpet and clarinet and we worked them into three cuts from the soundtrack album.

Charlie and co. ended up playing the main villains in the movie, as the notorious Wild West Circus of Crime. The Big Scene occurs in a huge circus tent on the outskirts of Deadwood. We are finally playing a gig that is going down a blast with the good folk of 1865 when Charlie, Jimmy and Paul attempt to rob the box office with hilarious consequences when they flood the circus and Deadwood. The special effects were all done by Gerry Anderson's Supermarionation puppet company. They still look pretty good to me and stand up alongside today's hi-tech nonsense. I do remember that we visited Gerry's base while he was working on the film and that Richard came away with Lady Penelope and Commander Shaw under his coat. I've just viewed *Out of Time* again for the first time in an age and come to the opinion that it would have been a really good movie if we hadn't been in it. Brigitte, Charlie and Gerry were all class acts.

We had two premieres, in London and Liverpool. The Queen and Prince Phillip came to the local one. What on earth they made of it, I have no idea although they were both very polite at the cast line-up afterwards. And I was over the moon to have Phil actually aske me, 'And which one are you?' The Sixties really were a different planet as I remember that the premiere brought the centre of London to a standstill as the cinema was besieged by over ten thousand fans. Can't remember too much about the Liverpool event as we were pretty blotto by the time we arrived having agreed to a promotion with Bell's whisky who stocked our Rolls for the drive up from London. I think Harold Wilson, Ken Dodd and Bessie Braddock were the main guests. It's a bit of a blur, still.

TODAY

I'd been looking forward to today for a long time. Over sixty years to be honest. My triumphant return to St Mary's College for boys, except now it's for girls too. They must have been nuts to ask me to give the Prize Giving Day speech. I know how to hold a grudge through the decades. Over the last few weeks I've been scribbling down venomous one-liners about the bastard teaching staff who attempted to kick all joy out of my life via their bizarre catholic cult. Prize Giving was to be held at Paddy's Wigwam this year rather than down the Phil where we used to suffer through the most boring night of the year. I'd been told to come to the school first and the Head would then drive me into town as the kids bussed it.

How strange it was to walk in through the old gates and into reception where I had reported ten thousand times before when turning up late each day. I looked at the clock above the main doorway and was a little disappointed in myself to find I was bang on time today. I was greeted by the Head himself who didn't really have much to say and seemed relieved to palm me off to the Head Boy and Girl for a tour of the school. They were a lot more chatty and fun as we wandered down the oddly familiar corridors. The polished wood of the windows and doors brought back memories of…the polished windows and doors. And then there were the religious statues. Mary, Joseph, Jesus and various saints, all life-size and looking down upon us with slightly disappointed expressions as if they knew we could do better if we would just try.

The Chemistry lab has been replaced with a Computer Zone. Probably as well considering the near accidents we had with sulphuric acid, quicksilver, Bunsen burners and live frogs. I was totally transported back to the Fifties on walking into the

Dining Hall. It was the clatter and chatter and echoes mainly, but also a huge jug of custard I saw one boy skimming the thick skin from. The teachers waved me over to join them at their tables but I chose instead to sit down with a group of peculiar looking students. They had the same look I must have given Elvis all those years ago so I broke the ice by suggesting they might want to play truant this afternoon rather than suffer through the Speech Day bollocks. A rude word always goes down well with everyone of school age. The school dinner was pretty much as I remembered it. Tasteless. Heading back to the Head's office it was a strange moment to see my portrait on one corridor wall alongside a scene of the crucifixion.

On the drive into town the Head remained silent throughout unless I asked him a question. So, by the time we were heading through Litherland I thought stuff him and enjoyed the sights. Disappointed to find the sausage factory had gone. When did that happen? I always enjoyed seeing the huge cutout of the happy pig with a fork and sausage over his shoulder on the factory wall. You could see it for miles. It was the Litherland landmark. I guess Time waits for no pig … or sausage. The Liver Building still shocks me today in its cleaned up state. I miss the soot black look we all grew up with. It gave it and the Liver Birds atop a certain gravitas, which clean can't come near. Up past the old cathedral and left onto Hope Street. The Head let me out at the steps to what I still call the new cathedral despite it being well over fifty years old now. I remember skipping school and watching it go up bit by bit over the years. Don't ask me why but I ran up the steps. All of them, and that's a lot of steps. I've been running up steps all my life and I was glad to find once I reached the top that I stopped puffing within minutes. It's a funny old/new place inside. I don't know where they found the architects of the Sixties but I wish they had left them there. It has all the charm of an aircraft hanger without the aircraft. A couple of St Mary's kids spotted me and came over to lead me to a backroom for tea and biscuits before the event began. They were funny kids who reminded me of Richard and myself way back. We were soon sharing jokes about the Head and other members of staff. The

Head arrived shortly after with some fellah I recognised off the telly but couldn't remember exactly where. He was introduced to me as the local MP for the Tory or Labour party. Might have been the Lib Dems or UKIP. He smiled as we shook hands, all the while looking over my shoulder to survey the room in case there was somebody more important he should be spending his valuable time with. Luckily, there was, a school governor or somesuch.

I sat in a corner and pulled out the notes for my speech. Lucky there was no naked light around as they were pretty inflammatory verging on downright nasty. I was sure the kids of the school would get a kick out of every barbed word. The kids of St Mary's past most certainly would be cheering me on. I underlined a few sentences to make sure I gave dramatic pauses and sudden loud outbursts full vent. This speech had been bubbling away and writing itself for over sixty years. I folded it up and slipped it into my inside jacket pocket as the Head called me to order for the opening procession. The full school and teaching staff were going to march round the aisles of the cathedral bearing flags of religious antiquity before taking our seats for the start of the proceedings. I fell in just behind the Head at the front of the line. There was already a full house of parents and grandparents. I got a couple of 'Hey, Mikey's' from various old boys of the school as we plodded round and round.

While the Head proceeded to the pulpit to deliver his opening speech, I sat down next to an ancient white haired chap three rows back. He nudged me in a familiar way, his eyes gleaming as he asked, 'Remember me, Mick?' I must have looked blank so he filled me in.

'Gordon Kelly. I sat behind you for two years in 1B and 2B.' I guess he would have looked different then back when we were twelve and thirteen but it was still shocking to realise we must be the same age. Hopefully my years of Pop and Rock Star privilege have held back Time. Looking at him he must have been doing sixteen hour shifts down a coal mine since our school years. As the Head droned on, Gordon waxed lyrical about our good old days.

'This guy's a bit of a dick but those old days weren't so bad, were they? We had some fun along the way. I come here every year. Don't know why really as it is always as boring as hell but then it always was, wasn't it? I suppose I'm here for the energy you can feel from the kids. Same as in our day. Doesn't matter about the Headmasters or teaching staff. It's all about the next generation, isn't it? I always hope they might be the ones to get it right. I mean, just look at their little faces.'

I looked round at the kids of the school and could understand how he felt. They all looked as bored out of their minds as we had at Prize Giving and Speech Days back in our schooldays but you could see something else lying dormant behind the glazed eyes. Energy, life, just as Gordon said.

'And it gives me great pleasure to welcome back to St Mary's College one of our most successful students, Mr Mike Simon...' The Head waved a hand for me to come and take his place at the pulpit. I pulled my notes from my inside pocket, stood up and walked down the aisle, shook his hand and climbed the four steps to the pulpit. What a strange thing to do. I realised that of all the many odd things I had done in my life, this was the first time I had stood in a pulpit looking down at a congregation. I laid my notes out in front of me and looked back at the assembled parents, grandparents, teachers, and children. The children's eyes seemed to glow. I looked over to Gordon who was smiling up at me and then back at the kids. They seemed expectant, waiting on my words of great wisdom. I skimmed over my notes. Poisonous words leapt off each page. Angry, negative, stupid, the words of a grumbling old git. Pointless venom aimed at men dead in their graves for over a quarter of a century. Men who were merely a product of their time. I looked up again at the children of today and tomorrow. Some of them were nudging each other in an attempt to bring on forbidden titters, aware that the old git up front was taking way too long to get started. I swept my hand across the pages of notes, letting them tumble slowly from the pulpit. I coughed to clear my throat and mind and began.

'I've been invited here today to give you an inspirational speech to set you up for a career as glittering and successful as mine. Well, I've just this minute realised I don't do inspirational speeches. But I do make a lovely cup of tea, and it's those cups of tea, sometimes with biscuits, that stand out in my life as golden moments much more than the gold discs and Daffodilmania. So, all I can suggest to you is to make sure on the day you leave school that you remember exactly who you were before you started on your first day in reception. It's your world. Do with it as you see fit.'

I was back to my seat before the tentative applause started and withered away quickly. The Head clambered back into the pulpit and thanked me grandly but I think he'd written his words before he had heard my speech. Gordon nudged me and winked.

'Short and sweet.'

YESTERDAY

In the early days, Mum would send me cuttings she meticulously snipped out of newspapers and magazines. Today one of them flittered out from a book I lifted up from a shelf. *The Saint in New York* is the Pan paperback, one of those 2/6 jobs to read on the tour bus. The cutting was from *Fabulous* weekly magazine which featured a colour pin-up of me beaming out at the world while holding up a toy giraffe. No idea why a giraffe, but, why not?

MIKE SIMON'S FAVOURITES
Colour: Black
Film: Whistle Down the Wind
Book: Telephone Directory
TV Show: The Epilogue
Actress: BB
Record: All I Want for Christmas is a Beatle
Sweet: Wine Gums
Food: Wine Gums
Drink: Ovaltine
Historical Character: Ug the Caveman
Sport: Conkers

YESTERDAY

EARLY SCHOOL MEMORY FROM OUT OF THE BLUE

St Mary's College, Crosby, in Liverpool did their very best to ensure their pupils would absolutely hate books for life on Friday 15th September in 1948. According to my Enid Blyton Diary for that year, that was the date the school had arranged for the visit of local author James Twatter. I kid you not about his name. For us primary school kids of the day it was a name he more than lived up to. According to the note we had been given to take home to our parents, Twatter would be giving us an insight into the heady world of publishing and revealing his own secrets of a successful writing career. He would also be giving us a reading from his latest picture book, *Sissy Goes to the Dentist*. This was the sixth in this particular series of books which followed Sissy the Bear as she went to the following locations:

Sissy Goes to School
Sissy Goes to Church
Sissy Goes to Hospital
Sissy Goes to the Shops
Sissy Goes to the Seaside

Neither myself or any of my classmates in Prelim had a single copy of any of the Sissy series. We would rather drink holy water and eat boot polish. The books were in the same dreadful vein as the Andy Pandy TV series, which always made me gag. Wet doesn't come close. Twatter made his first mistake that

75

September day by turning up. To my youthful eyes he looked old which probably means he was certainly over 25 years of age. He was dressed in Tweeds and carried an umbrella and a suitcase when he entered our classroom. His second mistake came when he referred to us as children in his greeting of "Hello, children". Having just turned eight, this was an out and out insult. His goose was well and truly cooked when he opened his suitcase to reveal Sissy herself. He proudly held her up and made her wave an arm at us. I swear that was the moment I first heard the phrase "FFS!" It came from Tony Cutler who sat next to me. He was a slightly rough child who came from across the tracks in Litherland near the dreaded Bootle. For us boys from the Southport end of Liverpool, Cutler was the closest we had to a borstal boy in our midst. Twatter then gave a talk all about his career as a writer. I still have the notes we were made to take down from his blether:

Still a boy at heart.
Always carries a pencil.
The idea for Sissy came to him in a pub.
All of his books have a moral.
Words are his friend.
Writing is all about hard work (As if!)
Already working on the next two Sissy books.

After his talk, Twatter said we could now have a Q&A session. Not a single hand went up so he went on to give a reading from *Sissy Goes to the Dentist*. The gist of the story was that Sissy had been scared to go to the dentist and so had stopped smiling to hide her rotting teeth. Through a series of rhyming incidents, Sissy learnt that the dentist was her friend and ended up with the shiniest teeth in town. While Twatter was reading this drivel out, Tony Cutler had been busy in his school jotter. He nudged me to show a drawing he had done of a book cover featuring Sissy going up in flames as the Devil poked her with his trident. The title of the book was *Sissy Goes to Hell*.

Our author's visit ended with Twatter having the gall to try and flog us his crappy books. "Only 3/6!" 3/6 was a small fortune to us kids back in 1961. Not a single buyer did he find, but he gave each of us a postcard listing the books in the Sissy series under the heading: JAMES TWATTER – AUTHOR. I remember getting home that day and telling Mum about the experience. She was incensed. "What a bloody cheek!" she erupted, slinging his card in the fire. "Author, indeed! He's a greengrocer in St John's Road!" Turned out that Twatter had his books printed in what used to be called a Vanity Publishing deal. Not too surprisingly, such deals have since reinvented themselves as Independent Publishers; usually independent of quality control.

Sadly, James Twatter, Author & Greengrocer, has no place in our modern world, not even as a footnote on the internet. I checked today.

YESTERDAY

It was a big deal when we were asked to appear on 'Sunday Night at the London Palladium'. You can have no idea how big that show was. Everybody had been on it. The biggest names from the US, Europe and the UK. Goodness knows how many millions of viewers. I guess it was our version of the 'Ed Sullivan Show'. We used to watch it back in the Fifties when it was hosted by Bruce Forsyth. Everybody but everybody loved the 'Beat the Clock' interlude they dropped in the middle of the show. Ordinary people from the audience given their moment of fame to beat the clock and win huge prizes like vacuum cleaners or the giddy amount of twenty-five pounds. Bruce and 'Beat the Clock' had gone by the time we topped the bill, and Liverpool's own Jimmy Tarbuck had taken over as the MC in the wake of Beatlemania. He had the moptop and cheeky wit. We were on the week after the Rolling Stones had refused to stand on the revolving stage at the end of the show to wave to the audience with the rest of the acts. This had caused huge controversy almost on the same scale as they had earned after pissing on a garage wall. The image they were carefully cultivating didn't do cute or cheesy. We, on the other hand, couldn't wait to ride that revolving stage and wave to our families back home. I say we topped the bill but my memory might be playing up because I do remember that Australia's Rolf Harris was also on the show that night. He was surely bigger than us at that time. He did his Jake the Peg three-legged bit and also painted a picture of the Aussie outback with huge paintbrushes. There was paint everywhere. We loved the Palladium. Slap bang in the heart of London, which for Liverpool boys meant we'd made it. Finally! It was our favourite theatre, even beating the Liverpool Empire, which held a special place in our hearts because that's where we'd seen pantomimes when we were kids. After Rolf, the rest of the bill comprised Alfredo, a strange chap from Europe who sat at his drum kit and spat and caught ping pong balls in his mouth as they rebounded from his snare, a little dog act, Arthur Haynes the comedian, and Cleo Laine. Music Hall was still alive and entertaining the masses. During rehearsals that afternoon, Arthur Askey dropped in. He was appearing in the theatre's panto that year and we had his dressing room. I remember we were quite awed in his presence. I mean, Arthur Askey! No bigger name to ever come out of Liverpool back in the Twenties. He was very funny and nice to us scruffs. He was very, what can I say, Arthur Askey. Big Hearted Arthur. I remember Richard asking him to do the Buzzy Bee song but he declined. Another memory of that day is of the Palladium sandwiches. I have no idea why they should stick in my memory over sixty years on but they do. Huge platters of them in the theatre Green Room. I should have taken a photo. It was a good show filled with good feeling. We loved riding the revolving stage at the end, job done. The Stones don't know what they missed. Decades later, Richard and I were asked to join that year's celebs on the BBC's 'Strictly Come Dancing'. Although we were still pretty nifty movers, we declined after much thought as we felt the show a little too cute and cheesy for our mature image. I kind of regret that now and think we should have gone on and had wild flings with our professional dance partners.

YESTERDAY

1st March 1968 – It's funny the people you meet at an airport. Richard and I were flying out to join The Beatles at the Maharishi's holiday camp in Rishikesh but as we strolled through the London airport, who do we see but Ringo and Maureen heading towards us from Arrivals.

'How come?' seemed the obvious question.

'Run out of Beans,' said the lugubrious one. We thought this must be some sky-high, inner meaning type answer from the cosmos, but, as it turned out, it meant what it said on the tin. Ringo had run out of his stock of Heinz finest product and, as he had a very dodgy stomach, he'd returned to the land of Tesco's Supermarkets rather than chance his luck with Indian fare.

So why exactly were we heading out to India? Simple. It was 1968. If you were there and you remember that year then you will know it was the time that Pop and Rock Stars came to the realisation that the Toppermost of the Poppermost wasn't all it was made out to be. In other words, we were all thinking, there must be something more than this. And then The Fabs found the Maharishi Mahesh Yogi with his advanced Transcendental Meditation, and it seemed like a good idea at the time.

TODAY

Email from Agent Orange attaching latest email from BINK Publishing commenting on my latest pages for autobio:

WHY ISN'T HE MENTIONING JANE? TRAGEDY SELLS.

There have been 3 times in my life when I have wondered if I had gone mad/insane/hadmentalissues or whatever the current term is for going stark staring bonkers. Reading those 2 lines, IN CAPITALS, was one of them. After the initial conflagration of screaming rage where I somehow hefted my computer screen through my office window, I sat on Jane's blue rug ('It'll last forever, like us.') and felt the breeze blow in through the smashed window. For the countless time in my life I came to the conclusion that I was a resident alien on this planet. The thought helped bring my pulse rate down and the dizziness to subside. Tragedy? Those stupid fuckers. Jane was never that. It's true that I haven't mentioned her so far in the book. I suppose that must seem strange as for 38 years we were MikeandJane. God knows, I still am. She still is. But where would I start to capture her? I should be able to walk into the living room and ask her that question, but, of course, I can't. Well, I do, but I get no answer. So maybe I should just start at the start like Mr Fitzgerald, my old primary school English teacher would instruct.

YESTERDAY

'Oi!'

That was my first word to Jane Gatewood. She never let me forget it.

'Who says Romance is dead?' she would say on every anniversary of that date: Tuesday 13th May 1986 at 6:35am. I was at Heathrow Airport to fly out to New York to help save Ethiopia or feed Africa or maybe it was an Aids benefit. Coming out of WH Smiths with a bagful of reading material for the flight, I saw her for the first time. She had a suitcase in each hand and a shoulder bag. She didn't notice as her scarf fell from her shoulders onto the ground behind her.

'Oi!'

That's how it all started. Yes, that's how my life started. Everything else that had happened up to that point falls into insignificance. She stopped, put her suitcases down, picked up the scarf and did the usual double-take as she realised who I was.

'Now there's a familiar face.'

I helped carry her bags to the nearby café and ordered 2 cups of tea.

'My first tea in England!' she was excited by the tea, not me.

'Heathrow hardly counts as England,' I told her.

She would later say that she knew at once. I certainly knew by the time we finished that tea. Africa would have to fend for itself. We got the tube to Tottenham Court Road, laughing all the way. I don't know why I chose the Y Hotel. Doesn't make sense all these years later. I guess you had to be there at the time. Luckily, we were.

TODAY

Richard rang. He never calls. Well, not since Crosby days. He asked me how I was. He's never done that, even back in the Crosby days. He's never asked how anyone is. I was dominating the conversation. He was providing the long pauses until….

'I've got cancer.'

I've lost count of how many people have told me that over the last ten years. Enough that it no longer has quite the effect it once did. There was a pause though to show I'm not a complete bastard before I clicked in with the Derek & Clive routine:

'Of the knob?'

No pause this time, he laughed, loud and long.

'I needed that. It is funny. As your Jane would have said, you've got to laugh.'

Sitting in Jane's chair in our living room with her ashes boxed in the undertaker's carrier bag on the table behind me, I had to agree.

'Anyway, before I drop dead I need to raise a ton of dough. Kids and wives, y'know.'

'Leaving your house in order?'

'Ha! Yeah, that will be a first, but yeah. So I was wondering if this tour you've been talking about could be changed to a Dream Daffodils reunion finalé tour.'

'Just the two of us?'

'Well, yeah, with your band and I suppose we could involve Laurence if we end up playing Falsom Prison.'

It was my time to laugh.

'How long have we got?'

'12 months tops.'

'Ok. I'll call Agent Orange. She'll be very happy.'

'Great. And thanks. But no old folks homes this time round.'

'Good idea. They probably wouldn't let us out.'

YESTERDAY

BE ONE OF THE BEAUTIFUL PEOPLE IN 1967 BY JOINING THE DREAM DAFFODILS FAN CLUB TODAY!

For the whole month of December 1966 the Dream Daffodils Fan Club is offering a full year membership for only 5/6! Yes, that's 5/6! Ask yourself the simple question: Can I afford not to join? You know the answer! Here's what you get:

Membership Card authorised by Mike Simon himself!

Two inch Dream Daffodils button badge!

Four glossy pin-ups of the boys. These shots available only through the Fan Club!

Newsletter - inside info on all upcoming Daffodil news!

Giant FULL COLOUR poster of the band taken on stage at their recent Royal Variety Show appearance.

Signed copy of *Twelve Children and It*, Laurence's upcoming kids' book!

Don't delay, send today!

Send a postal order for 5/6 made out to the Dream Daffodils Fan Club at the address below.

My main memory of the Dream Daffodils Fan Club is that the club secretary, Beverly Grimshaw absconded in 1968 with £33,000 worth of postal orders.

YESTERDAY

Jane Gatewood did eventually interview me. She'd been interviewing Pop and Rock stars since the day she turned fourteen back in 1964. Her first interview question to me had been the unique:

'Do you have a tree house?'

That certainly beat will the Dream Daffodils ever play together again?

Jane's life had been changed that February night in 1964 by Ed Sullivan. Her hometown of Indianapolis was slap bang in the centre of all forthcoming tours by the British Invasion. Recognising this, Jane put a call in to the editor of one of the current most popular teen mags out of New York. In her most grown up voice she told him:

'I have an interview with those English pop stars Peter and Gordon. Would you be interested in running it?'

Jane always claimed that was one of only two lies she told in her life. It being 1964 when anything Pop and English sold in the millions, the editor signed Jane up, interview unseen. This allowed Jane to contact Peter and Gordon's management and ask:

'I'm a correspondent with Tiger Beat. We're very interested in interviewing your boys Peter and Gordon when their tour reaches Indianapolis. Can you arrange this?'

They can and they did.

Jane was met by Peter Asher in the lobby of their hotel in downtown Indianapolis.

'Hello, Jane. Come on up to our room. It will be cosier there.'

As this was 1964 and Jane had just turned fourteen, no alarm bells rang here. Up in their room, Peter introduced Jane to Gordon Waller.

''Let's do the interview on the bed,' he suggested.

Laying between the two suited and booted Pop Stars, Jane opened her notebook, licked her pencil tip and asked Peter:

''Is your sister Jane's hair as blazingly red as yours?'

That was the first of tens of thousands of quirky questions Jane would go on to ask the world's greatest Rockers during her lifetime.

At the end of the interview, Peter suggested:

'Don't rush off, Jane. We've got something here you might enjoy.'

Walking over to the television set, he turned it on and for the next two hours the trio lay on the bed together watching *Bonanza* and *The Wonderful World of Disney*. And that was Jane Gatewood's entry into the heady world of sex, drugs and Rock and Roll.

TODAY

Agent Orange calls first thing all excited to announce that she's sending a car to pick up Richard and me to take us to the BBC TV Centre in Salford to announce that the Dream Daffodils are back and will be on tour with a new album.

'What album?' I ask.

'Oh you'll both come up with something. You've got time.'

'The only time Richard's got is borrowed. Have you seen the state of him?'

'Stop worrying about details, Michael. That's why you have an agent.'

'Okay. I'll tell Death that, should I?'

Richard seemed to have rallied on the drive to Salford. He actually looked good, which is a miracle at this age, particularly with cancer No. 4. He spent most of the time chatting up our driver, a busty Scottish girl who'd never heard of us but seemed up for a good time, however unlikely that would be in Salford.

Reporting to reception at the BBC's Quay House there was some confusion as it seemed nobody was expecting us. We'd assumed we were going on a news show. The problem was cleared up when a bright young thing (gender unspecific) pranced up to us and explained we were in the wrong building.

'You're with CBeebies, next door, dearies.'

'What the fuck are we doing on CBeebies?' asked Richard.

'You're on the Bach Sisters show, *Musical Alphabet*,' he/she/it told us.

I'll admit that even after all Richard and I had been through since the Fifties, there was a stunned pause at this news. Richard was the first to break it.

'We could storm off but life's too short. At least mine is.'

'Remind me to get us a new agent on Monday.'

We were led to the CBeebies studio where the Bach twins greeted us like long lost soulmates. They were both dressed in rainbow colours as was the set for their show.

'So, so, so good to see you both,' they squawked, giving us one of their neverending hugs. 'And it is perfect timing. Today we shall be telling children about the letter D in music.'

'D?' asked Richard.

'D for Dream Daffodils,' they both sang.

'What's your target audience for this show?' I asked.

'The under fives,' the girls smiled.

Richard and I looked at each other, deliberated on doing a Keith Moon on the studio set, but instead burst out laughing. It was the first time we'd really laughed together since … well, in a long time.

'I can see our tour now…' I gasped between laughter. 'Stadiums full of under fives.'

'Our core audience,' said Richard.

God knows what that core audience made of our tour announcement in the middle of the Twins' show, but then God hopefully also knows what those CBeebies babies made of the whole of the show. While drawing the letter 'D' on a blackboard 100 times, Richard and I had to enunciate the same letter the same number of times but making sure each time we said it we used a different tone. There was a child therapist off set who explained to us how this would stimulate learning in those under fives. Complete bollocks, of course. On the ride home we were quite amazed at ourselves for having gone along with the nonsense of the twenty-first century for the very first time. Happily, when the show aired the following day, our expressions said everything.

YESTERDAY

Clipping from *Disc* newspaper 13th January 1968:

TAKE YOU TO PLEASURELAND
Dream Daffodils follow up to chart smashing *That's Me Inside You* is another guaranteed No. 1 from the Liverpool boys. Simon & Macadam's trademark suggestive lyrics might well get the BBC's puritan knickers in a twist but their banning of the record will only make it even more of a must-buy for the band's global audience. Mike Simon's vocals will be looked on as *The Sound of 1968* by future music historians. B-Side: *Touch Me There* turns up the heat and is the first time the word nipple has appeared on a record. There's no question, this disc will keep Dream Daffodils fans coming.

DREAM DAFFODILS MONTHLY NOW ON SALE!
The only official Dream Daffodils magazine is available from all newsagents on the first Thursday of every month. Keep up to date with all DD news as it happens. This month Mike Simon exclusive as he tells you all about his Christmas and plans for 1968. Behind the scenes photos! Only 2/6d!

YESTERDAY

I've often wondered why we headed out to India in 1968. It's just so not us. I guess that just like the Beatles by that time we had reached the Toppermost of the Poppermost and found much to our surprise that there wasn't anything there besides money and girls. Nothing wrong with money and girls, of course, but by 1968 everyone from Billy Graham to Charles Manson were chasing the spiritual side of life. Billy and Charlie certainly weren't what we were after. Nor was the Maharishi as it turned out. We sat through one class with him. Laurence fell asleep. Well, it had been a long flight to get there and we'd come direct after a world tour. From what I can remember the class was about connecting yourself to an insect.

'We are mere grubs but our souls can be connected to the Great Source of the Living Energy that lights up the universe within.'

Richard leaned close to me as we sat cross-legged at the master's feet.

'Bloody rubbish this,' he whispered, recalling our gig at the old folk's home back in Crosby. Jet-lagged myself, I laughed out loud, interrupting the Maharishi's train of thought. His piercing eyes looked direct into my excuse for a soul.

'Laughter is good … for a grub.'

That was it for the entertainment and the food was even worse. None of us were into spice. I haven't had another curry since '68. Laurence turned out to be the only one who enjoyed his time in India. On that first night, he found Lava, a very pretty Indian girl who looked about 8 years of age. She was an orphan living on the streets and her wits outside the Maharishi's compound. Her wits bagged her a Dream Daffodil as she left with us two days later.

'She's 18,' said Laurence.

Yeah, right!

'Going on 6,' replied Richard.

I was woken on our last day at the compound as cries of 'cunt', 'fuck', 'shit', 'twat' and 'motherfucker' disturbed the serenity of the place. Heading out of my Butlin's like chalet I found Richard and Mike Love of the Beach Boys kicking the crap out of each other in the dining area. Mike's snow white kaftan was already covered in blood from his streaming nose. It was a long and bitter battle and I'd finished two rounds of toast, fish and orange juice and two cups of tea before it ground to a halt as the debauched bodies of the rock stars could take no more. Richard came over and collapsed on the chair next to mine.

'What was that all about?'

'I just don't like the Beach Boys,' explained Richard. So much for spiritual awareness.

Before we left, the Maharishi gave us an envelope each. Inside was our own personal mantra plus a bill for food, lodgings and lessons. I remember my mantra to this day. When I had it translated it read:

Everything you know is illusion so know nothing.

Very helpful, I'm sure.

YESTERDAY

Sid Vicious gobbed in my face while we were sharing a lift at the BBC TV Theatre in Shepherd's Bush. It was either 1978 or '79, definitely some time after the Pistols set-to with Bill Grundy when the band became the three hundred and fifty-fifth people to swear on British television. I'm not sure what we were doing there. *The Generation Game*? Unlikely. We'd been sharing a dressing room with Billy J Kramer. Oddly, this was the first time I'd actually met Billy and so, inevitably, our chat turned to Liverpool memories and folk we'd met along the way. Sid just sat slumped in a corner, swigging something from a large bottle. I don't know what it was he was drinking but it was green and obnoxious, like him. As Billy and I reminisced, Sid would interject every now again with a slurred 'wankers' or 'for fuck's sake' or 'knobheads'. We ignored the little rodent, contenting ourselves with the odd look heavenwards when he started pissing in the dressing room sink. It became obvious to us both that the Pop World was changing from the days of the Partridge Family and the Osmonds. Now it was the Sex Pistols and the Nolans. After whatever show we were on I found myself going up or down in the lift when Sid let rip. I say gobbed, it could well have been puked. It was certainly green against my crisp white shirt. I have no idea whether it was intended as some kind of one-upmanship masterplan by Sid or just an involuntary reaction of his body to his daily diet, but it was very effective in bringing my usually buried Mr Hyde personality to the fore. As the lift doors opened we were both struggling on the ground, Sid's balls crunching in my iron grip. To add to the surreal quality of the scene, Queen Elizabeth II and her husband Prince Phillip, the Duke of Edinburgh, were standing in the foyer looking down at us. My main memory of what happened next is of a thousand press photographers' flash-bulbs popping. Sid and I covered the front pages the following morning. On the bright side, the Pistols and I were in the top five the following Sunday. Say what you like about Sid but he took the time to send me a 'Fuck you' card shortly afterwards.

TODAY

We'd been in the studio for two weeks, plonking away on new songs. The problem was that the new songs sounded remarkably like our old songs but not as good.

'I've come to the conclusion that we are well and truly has-beens,' declared Richard over our sixth coffee of the day.

'We used to be inspired, now we're sad and tired,' I quoted from Jesus Christ Superstar.

'Listening to this crap is certainly crucifying,'

'Great news, boys! Great news!' It was Agent Orange breezing into the studio canteen. 'The concert dates are piling in like no tour before it. Every venue wants you and are fighting to get you! But the really big news of the day is that CBeebies are offering you a series of your own. I say your own but you'd be co-starring.'

'I'm not working with the twins!'

'No, no. The BBC are bringing back Lenny the Lion and they think it would make a great team-up in a series looking at mental and gender issues and how they relate to music.'

'On CBeebies?'

'Yes.'

'For kids?'

'Yes.'

I'm not sure whether it was Richard or myself who replied with the 'For fuck's sake!', possibly we duetted.

'Give it some thought,' suggested Orange. 'You've always said you need the younger audience.'

'Not the fucking under fives!'

'So how's the album going? We really need it for the tour. Have you thought of the design and cover shot? And what are we going to call it?'

'At the moment we're calling it Bollocks,' I replied.

'Really? Well we can't have that. Looks like I'm back just in time,' came a familiar voice from behind us. We turned to find a beaming Laurence walking towards us, tea cup in hand.

'Who let you out?' asked Richard.

Laurence explained that he had been released early on good behaviour which made us all laugh considering what he had been banged up for in the first place. We thought prison overcrowding being the more likely reason.

'I've got so many ideas for the album,' he told us. 'Not a lot else to do inside.'

Laurence certainly did have a lot of ideas for the album, each one as bad as our own. By midnight we knew we were in trouble.

'I suppose we could do covers,' suggested Richard.

'What, Taylor Swift's greatest hits?' I snorted. 'No, thank you. We haven't done a cover since our second album.'

'We could do what the Fabs did back in '95,' said Laurence. 'When they realised their songwriting days were in the past they looked into their archives and pulled out all the stuff they'd rejected first time round. *Anthology*, that's it. Made a mint.'

Our relief was palpable. Album done. Richard even came up with the title, *Rejects*.

'Triple album at least,' laughed Richard.

'Variant covers for completists,' agreed Laurence.

'Mono and stereo releases,' I let the pound signs dance in my head. 'I guess we've finally sold out.'

'Pff! We sold out in '67,' said Richard. 'The fucking Dream Daffodils, for God's sake!'

YESTERDAY

I saw my first nude woman the day after I turned fourteen. This was a truly cosmic event in my life. There had been no nudity in Liverpool before this magnificent day. Well, unless you count the school showers in Chesterfield Road after bloody horrible Games Days. There had been a flurry of interest there two years before on the first spotting of pubic hair. That was on Jim Foster, a rather hirsute boy who was regularly sent home to shave after the age of eleven. No, I don't count the showers in Chesterfield Road. My first nude woman was named Miss April and she appeared over eight pages of a magazine called *Playboy* in the glorious year of 1954. Pages 125-133. Five of the pages were in full glossy colour, including the fold-out, a particularly titillating pose that captured tits and ass and a half smile that promised a life I couldn't even imagine. She was five foot four inches tall, brunette, from Oregon, drove a Volkswagon, was nineteen years of age, and wanted to break into Hollywood.

To me she was the most beautiful thing I'd ever seen in my life. I used to dream about her in Latin class. For that fourteen year old kid, *Playboy* was the epitome of glamour. It represented unreachable America. A dream world, far removed from the bombsite that was still Merseyside. The magazine had cost me an arm and a leg from the school spiv, Tony Gallagher, a 6th former. Goodness knows where he got it from. He also offered me a pair of nylons at the same time. The World War Two black market was still in operation at St Mary's College. Miss April 1954 would be in her nineties now. I hope she made it to Hollywood. She certainly brought great pleasure to me. I'm still a fan. It was probably because of Miss April that I was so over the moon when the Dream Daffodils duly got a major interview in Playboy back in January 1969. We'd done the interview at the Playboy Mansion in LA, where we met Hugh Hefner who was everything you'd want him to be, complete with smoking jacket, cravat and Barbie Benton, his current bride. That issue meant a lot to me. It's still on the shelf in our living room. The fourteen year old kid inside me couldn't believe his luck. By 1973 women's liberation was kicking in and *Playgirl* had joined *Playboy* on the top shelf at WH Smiths. I laughed for a week when the editor approached me to be Mr April (of all months!) that year. Of course, there was no way my ego would allow me to refuse, but I did check myself out from all angles in a full-length mirror before accepting. It was all tastefully done and they had bedecked the whole studio with about ten thousand daffodils for me to lay amongst for the fold-out shot. I think I peaked that day. I caught sight of myself in that same full-length mirror the other day on the way from shower to dressing. The sight stopped me in my tracks. Mr April 1973 now has tits to compete with Miss April 1954.

YESTERDAY

Richard and I were on a plane going somewhere neither of us can remember when we first saw our Prime Minister Theresa May dancing to the old Dream Daffodils hit *Inside Outside*. She wasn't on the plane but rather on a news channel we were tuned into. She was at a Tory party conference if I remember correctly and the members (for want of a better word) clapped along ecstatically. We thought it was hilarious. Number one, she couldn't dance to save her life, and, number two, the song had been inspired by a question Richard had been asking with new sex partners since his teens. Theresa obviously thought she looked great because she adopted the song as her signature tune for all future events. That's when we got hammered. Political nitwits starting asking the question, why didn't we object to her using the song? Could we possibly be, dare I say it, Conservatives?

The simple reason we didn't object is because we didn't give a toss. We've never been political in the least. We think they are all cunts with a capital 'C'. If anything, we wanted Mrs May to carry on making a mug of herself to our soundtrack. Anyway, it was probably because of our silence that I found myself up for a knighthood at the next year's honours list. That's kind of how Great Britain works politically. The letter from Downing Street claimed it was for my service to the culture of the country but I find that hard to believe. Culture? Give me a break! Of course I chose to accept. I had two main reasons. One, to piss off all anti royalists who I've always found to be such an irritating little bunch of whiners who can't do the simple math of deducing they are in a minority. And number two, because it's so fucking insane. Sir Mike Simon for crying out loud! It's a bit like being told you are now Captain America.

The letter from Buckingham Palace duly arrived. The sheen was taken off the gilt somewhat by the final lines which read: 'For this week only we can offer you a video cassette of your presentation to Her Majesty at the amazing price of only £49:50. Please send cheque by return of post to guarantee this one-time only service.' Reading it, I sat drinking my breakfast tea, pondering on whether to be angry or entertained by such blatant money making bollocks. I mean, my country is honouring me but only at a cost to myself of £49:50. I think it was the fifty pence that got me. In the end I decided to be entertained. Not for the first time I came to the conclusion that everything in life is a joke. And Jane insisted that I deserved it.

'Think ahead. You can always do a Lennon and send it back to promote a future cause.' A fair point. Also, as an American she fancied going to the palace. And so we did. It ended up being our final trip out together apart from to countless hospitals in the following years. As final trips go it was fun. Her Majesty, despite rumour to the contrary, had a lot to say, to us both, which was nice. She reminded us of my Mum. Same generation, I guess. And she knew her stuff. She rattled off the names of several Dream Daffodils songs. Even I'd forgotten them. That's putting in the homework for you.

'You know our songs?' I asked in amazement.

'Of course I do!' she replied, just holding back from adding Captain Mainwaring's irritable 'stupid boy'.

I was given a medal and ribbon in a red plush box during the ceremony. The actual knighting with the sword took me back to tales of Sir Lancelot that I had loved so much as a child. I told the Queen that all I needed now was a round table.

'You could try John Lewis. The sales are on.' She deadpanned.

On the way home, I gave Jane the medal, ribbon and box. Quite right too.

YESTERDAY

Everybody was moaning about lockdown in 2020. Not us. Jane and I were more than happy to lock the world outside our front door. Us. That's all we'd ever really wanted. It was wonderful to be at home rather than in a hospital. By then we'd had 19 years of Jane's health issues. All had been well until that optician had suggested after an eye check that Jane go to the hospital and insist on getting an MRI scan. A week later we were standing in a specialist's office as he pointed to the x-ray of Jane's brain on a lit screen.

'The tumour has been growing for twenty years. Unfortunately it has grown round the carotid artery so we won't be able to take the whole thing out. You will be blind by Christmas if we don't operate quickly. It is a dangerous operation. Mr Simon, please go and lie down on the gurney. You are about to pass out.'

As I stretched out, a nurse came into the room and did a double-take from me to Jane. She obviously thought she'd got the patents mixed up.

'So what do we do?' asked Jane, all business. The specialist outlined a hellish plan. Getting home that evening, we sat amongst the familiar things in our downstairs kitchen and both burst into tears. Choking back our new reality, Jane wiped a tear from my face and smiled.

'You've got to laugh.'

We would repeat that line countless times over the next 19 years. God, I miss her.

TODAY

The Bach Twins are number one. It says so on their website. The small print reveals that they are number one in something called *The Indie North West Remote Autistic Children's Chart*. I don't think we had that back in the Fifties when we started. Grand celebrations on the Twins' Facebook and website with 40% off all merchandising. That reminds us we have to get a suitable cover shot for the new album.

It was Laurence's idea to dress the 3 of us in surviving costumes we'd worn through the glory years. We'd all remained reasonably trim thanks to cancer or life so little retailoring would be necessary. Pretty much everything had been kept in storage since those years as we had once had the idea of creating a musical museum full of the detritus of the business. Clothes, contracts, photos, guitars, posters, and set lists were all there. It was like a Tutankhamen's tomb of bad taste. We had a selection of costumes brought over. Richard chose the Epstein leathers from McCartney's 21st birthday while Laurence squeezed into a 1965 suit. I went for the full psychedelic Daffodil look from 1967. The only changes we made were to the trousers which all needed 1950s turn-ups. In our eighties we were obviously all shrinking.

Orange arrived with new posters for the tour. Lost in the small print at the bottom of the page were the words: WITH SPECIAL GUESTS THE BACH TWINS! When I erupted she pointed out that Laurence had okayed it. Bloody typical although I would have thought they were a bit old for him. To be honest, I couldn't be bothered arguing the point. And, after all, it will pull in all the autistic kids from the North West.

We did a night shoot for the album cover and it went well. Togged out in our old gear we posed in Fleet Street outside Ye Olde Cheshire Cheese Pub beside a Mini car, black cab, and

Sixties MG from Richard's garage. 1000 shots taken in 30 minutes and we chose the winning entry over a pint or three in the pub. It was a striking shot although I'm a little worried we're entering Austen Powers territory thanks to all the Sixties references. Aww, what the Hell. It's only Rock & Roll as a wise man once said.

YESTERDAYS

Some memories have now combined and fused together as though they occurred on a single day. Butlins Holiday Camp and the White House are a good example of this. According to Daffodil biographies we were performing at Butlins in Pwllheli for a whole month back in 1964 but I can only remember a single moment standing on stage in their main ballroom as a drunk threw a full beer bottle directly at me. I felt its speed and force as it missed my head by a fraction to explode with force into Richard's forehead. He still has the scar. He was out for a good five minutes. I have no memory about what happened to the arsehole. That is my single Butlins moment in memory. We were pretty much unknown back then. Speed on many years and Richard and I are performing at a charity gig at the White House in Washington in front of the Obamas and selected guests. I forget the charity. There were so many over the years. The producer was a lovely guy named Dalton Delan. You can't beat a name like that. There were other names on the bill that night. Neil Young, maybe? I seem to remember Joan Baez. But my main memory comes from the afternoon rehearsal when a lighting tree collapsed and I was hit on the head by a huge backlight. I remember coming to, looking up at the White House ceiling. Very ornate. And then Richard's beaming face as he commented:

'This is just like being back at Butlins Holiday Camp!'

I also have the scar to this day.

YESTERDAY

Sitting here today, it's very strange looking through old boxes of diaries and journals to see just how much we crammed into each year. 1967 is beyond belief. There doesn't seem to be a second where we aren't running at breakneck speed. I'd completely forgotten about Joe Orton until I uncovered this script. Joe was The playwright of that mid Sixties period. His plays shocked and rocked and outraged audiences. We'd heard that Epstein (Brian not Jeffrey) had said no to Joe's film script for the Beatles because it turned the band into murderers. Pre Manson that kind of thought appealed to us and so we approached Joe to write what would be our second feature film. Yeah, that's the one that didn't get made. Well, it did get made, but...

Flicking through the script now I see that the whole film is set in a gentlemen's public toilet, which, apparently, is where Joe spent many of his waking hours. Word got out about the content of the script and we found ourselves banned in Alabama and Iran. Ala(be praised)bama works in mysterious ways causing Joe to be murdered by his boyfriend before the script was complete, and so we ended up writing the movie ourselves. It has to be said that as screenwriters we were right up there with McCartney's *Mystery Tour* and *Broad Street* efforts. The movie was part sci fi, part Western, part historical romance, part spy thriller. Add all the parts together and you get 100% bollocks. Speaking of which, one of our guest stars in the movie was Patrick Macnee, John Steed himself from *Avengers* fame. When we signed him up, he kindly invited us over to his house in Hollywood to a drinks party one afternoon in the Summer of Love. He answered the door stark bollock naked. The funny thing is that I don't remember this even registering on us at that moment. By that time in our success we spent a good time of each day naked ourselves. Turned out Pat was a nudist, unbeknown to all *Avengers* fans. He was a hoot, inviting us in to his huge pad. There were about 100 other people already there. We were the only ones clothed … for the first ten minutes. The other guests were mostly recognisable from movies and TV Westerns or sit-coms. Pat's co-star, Linda Thorson, was also there. She's the one with the eyes, remember? Tara King. She picked up an ornament from a shelf and turned those eyes on me.

'Isn't this lovely, darling? It's Peter Pan.'

It was those eyes rather than Peter that generated my immediate erection. This immediately changed the course of the conversation.

'Of course, darling, I was born thinking about sex. I was seven years of age when I realised how much I enjoyed touching myself. You know, down there. No! I tell a lie. I was eight. Even then I knew I had a good bottom.'

What can I say? The Sixties. You had to be there to believe it.

The movie was made in two weeks. The final edit could do with a final edit in the dumpster. Bootlegs are available unfortunately. I have heard the film described as being ahead of its time by various rabid fans. If so, I hope I don't live long enough to reach its time period. Here's a typical scene….

The band stand on a barren planet landscape. They are all wearing spacesuits except for Richard who is in t-shirt and underpants. Earth can be seen in the sky above.

Laurence: So whose idea was it to buy this dump?

Mike: Another few years and this will be prime real estate, man.

Richard: Has anyone seen Mickey Mouse?

Mickey walks into the scene, waving.

Mickey: Here I am, Richard!

500 nuns on motorbikes roar across the landscape. After they disappear over the horizon and the sound of the motors fade, close-up on Mike.

Mike: That reminds me, I must pick up some milk.

As I said, you had to be there. It says something about us that we had the good sense not to release it. Sometimes censorship can be a good thing.

TODAY

Off to the old BBC TV Centre first thing this morning for an appearance on ITV's *This Morning*. I've always hated the show. It's one of those ghastly things that when you first watch it you wonder how on earth it managed to get on the air in the first place; and then it goes and runs for decade after decade. Several hours of chat every weekday morning for over 30 years without anything of note actually being said. Quite an achievement. I guess it sums up our glorious modern world. Richard hates it even more than I do. He looks like death cooled off in the car to the studios today.

'Just so long as we're not being interviewed by that tosser Dermot or that hideous laughing hyena Alison,' he bellyached.

'Oh, I like her,' said Laurence, just to wind him up. 'According to Minx magazine she's dyslexic, so you have to give her her due. She's done very well considering.'

'For fuck's sake! Is there any celebrity who isn't dyslexic these days?' asked Richard taking a handful of god knows what pills.

Life being what it is, it was, of course the tosser and the hyena who were today's presenters. They greeted us with hugs like long lost relatives.

'Gerroff!' bellowed Richard, shoving Alison over onto the set couch.

'Don't worry about him,' said Laurence. 'He's just racist.' Hyena laugh from the hyena. Our interview came in the last half hour of the programme but some production idiot thought it would be a good idea to have us sat on the sofa throughout, commenting on each item. These items included:

1. A 15 year-old girl whose drink had been spiked at a concert.

2. The right kind of handbag to wear for the coming Autumn.

3. A politician who wants to bring back National Service for all 18 year-olds to cut down on knife crime and gangs of kids hanging round on street corners.

4. Which wheelchair gives best value?

5. Should transexuals be allowed to use public toilets?

We were fast losing the will to live by the time our spot came round. The fact that chummy Dermot was referring to each of us as 'mate' didn't help. The in-depth interview included the following questions:

1. How are you? You're looking good.

2. Will you ever retire?

3. Did you ever think you'd still be here back in 1957?

4. Who came up with the name Dream Daffodils?

5. Is it still fun?

6. Do you have a favourite song?

7. Would you support National Service?

Our answers were to the point:

1. Yes.

2. No.

3. Yes.

4. Aunty Doris.

5. Not at this moment.

6. No.

7. Only for politicians.

Richard finished off by calling Dermot a cunt, which achieved front page coverage in the evening papers. We've still got that old abusive magic.

YESTERDAY

I stopped opening the sympathy cards exactly two weeks after Jane died. I couldn't take the pastel colours and nightmarish Maya Angelou quotes any more. People kept assuring me that time was a great healer and that my memories would help sustain me. And worse, they started telling me that Jane would want me to be happy and live life to its fullest. Utter bollocks, of course. I knew Jane would be looking at her watch and asking the question:

'What's keeping you?' She was never one for procrastination. I have no idea what's keeping me. What's left of me. There's nothing here. I'm empty. Hollow. My heart has gone. I don't know why I'm still conscious. The pain is crippling. One pointless day after the next. I have no point to my existence. In every 24 hours I wake five or six times from naps. Each time it takes to the count of three before my new reality hits. That pain increases with each nap. It's now 26 weeks and counting. An idiot DJ called to ask me:

'Are you back to normal yet?'

Twat.

My first and last thought each day is that I wish I was dead. That thought crosses my mind several times during the day and night too. I am the undead. And so I attempt to fill my day with these stupid fucking projects. Album, tour, interview, hoovering, dusting, mowing, gardening, sweeping, reading, telly. Tick Tock into a new season. Why are the plants growing? Why am I pouring only one cup of tea. I just hate .... everything.

TODOY

'DOES THE NAME JOHN MEAN ANYTHING TO ANYONE HERE?'

I think I have finally lost my mind after the last 2 months of ghastliness for today I decided to attend a local Spiritualist Church. I was met at the door by a group of people all wearing Covid masks. It was like stepping back 5 years into the past. They handed me one and told me I could take it off once seated in the church.

The church hall was full of people looking as miserable as myself. A pall of grief hung over the room. This wasn't helped by the ceremony kicking off with 2 hymns I haven't heard since schooldays. Far from uplifting, they spoke of mans' sorrow and hardships. My heart sank when the medium for the evening introduced himself. He looked as if he had just stepped off Blackpool's North Pier back in the 1940s. And wouldn't you know it, his shtick was to perform as a comedic medium.

'By gum! They told me I'd be playing to Richmond's finest. Have I come to the wrong venue?'

Polite titter from the organiser.

'Reet then, let's get started. Does the name John mean anything to anyone here?'

Silence from the crowd until a wife nudges her husband and whispers: 'That could be John.'

The medium picks up on this.

'He passed over some time ago now. He's a bright chap about my height. He has a sweet tooth. Always liked to have a packet of Werthers in his pocket. Is that reet?'

The woman looks unsure.

'No, maybe it's Licorice Allsorts?' Still nothing from the woman.

'Back when he was a kid. He loved Licorice Allsorts.'

The woman flickers into life. 'Oh yes, yes, that could be him.'

'He liked clothes. He's showing me a dress jacket he's very proud of. And a betting slip. Did he like the horses?'

The woman looks lost again.

'Not all the time. Just when he got a good tip say on the National or the Derby.'

'Oh yes, yes.'

'Well he says to tell you he's okay and to stop worrying.'

Woman: 'Thank you.'

'Lady in the green coat. There's a woman on the other side. She passed with cancer. Does that mean anything to you?'

Woman in green: 'Oh, yes.'

'She's a tiny woman. Very small.'

'Oh, no. This was a big woman.'

'Well, of course, on the other side you can be any size you want. She's holding up a handbag. Did she have a handbag?'

'Yes, yes she did.'

'She knew her own mind.'

'Er...yes. I suppose so.'

'She had a wedding ring and a watch.'

'Yes, that's her.'

And so it went on and on and on. Jane had obviously got better plans for the evening and didn't turn up. I was hoping my grandfather might come through and give the medium a characteristic bollocking. But no. I didn't stop for tea and biscuits but made my way home through the gloom to our beautiful old house where Jane still shines through.

TODAY

'Okay, we need to figure out ticket prices for this tour. We're labelling it as the final tour so we should capitalise on that.' Orange was holding court in her office with the three of us. I was in an argumentative mood.

'For nostalgia's sake why don't we charge the same prices we charged at our first gigs?'

'What, sixpence?' smiled Laurence.

'We're not doing that simply cos we're not nostalgic,' Richard pointed out.

'What about tickets at half a crown? Two and six? That's what I paid when I saw Buddy Holly at the Phil.' Laurence again.

'McCartney and the Stones start their ticket prices from £250 for their latest tours,' said Orange, trying to knock some financial sense into us. 'So I'm thinking let's start this final tour prices from £500.'

'So it'll be a sell-out tour in more ways than one,' I protested.

'Actually, that would be a hoot.' Both Laurence and Richard were in agreement.

'Agreed then,' said Orange. 'Now onto merch. The Bach Twins can advise us there.' As if on cue the girls walked into the office carrying a dustbin between them. The bin was overflowing with Twin merchandise garbage. After hugs and kisses all round and a token sieg heil salute from Richard the twins emptied the bin on the floor in front of us.

'This is where the money is,' explained Orange. 'Just picture Dream Daffodil t-shirts, coffee mugs, hoodies, dressing gowns, pajamas, toddler wear, duvets, towels and tablecloths. Everybody will want to take home a souvenir.

'The bin's the right place for this crap,' I moaned. Of course the merch idea was carried two to one. But what do I care? I try and remind myself that originally we got into this business for two simple reasons: money and birds. Love of music definitely came third on that list.

YESTERDAY

13 July 1985

Live Aid was a hoot apart from one thing. Geldof. We took against him from the start. It was probably the accent. It was the spit of our old nemesis from schooldays, Brother Brickley who had gone out of his way to ensure we would never be able to play guitar by attempting to break our wrists with his savage handling of the deadly strap.

'What a twat!' Richard had said at the time about Brickley and that had been our instant reaction on first meeting with Bob. It didn't help that he opened the conversation with:

'I've always wondered who came up with such a fucking awful name as the Dream Daffodils? Anyway, you're playing at the JFK Stadium in Philadelphia on the 13th of July for my Live Aid concert. You can't say no. It's for starving kids so you would look real shits if you say you're busy.'

We've never had a problem helping starving kids but helping Bob was another thing. We deliberated for a week but when we heard Dylan was on the same bill we signed up. Dylan is one of those people who live up to their reputation. Unsmiling. Unfriendly. We loved him. Geldof introduced us via satellite tv link-up from London as we met in the JFK Green Room.

'Bob, the Dream Daffodils.'

'I know who they are, man. They inspired one of my songs.'

This was news to us.

'Really, which one?'

'Everything is Broken'.

We decided to take that as a compliment without interrogating further.

'Great song,' nodded Richard.

When Geldof left to go and swear at the public for not donating even more money, we sat on the Green Room sofa with Bob. We were all swigging the new Cherry Coke. Bloody awful stuff. Bob stared off into space as we desperately tried to come up with suitable conversation. Nothing we said registered enough to bring Bob back from the centre of his universe until I hit on Farm Aid.

'Did I hear a rumour you're doing something for the farmers of America?'

Bob instantly came to life.

'Yeah, that's who we need to be helping. The banks are foreclosing on broke farmers all across the country.' Bob spent the next twenty minutes going into great detail about the problem of farming in the USA. Realising this could be a great way to rattle Geldof's cage, Richard suggested:

'You should get Geldof to donate some of tonight's takings to the farmers. There's more than enough to go round.'

'Great idea, man.'

We watched in delight a little while later as Bob put this idea to Geldof via satelite. The resulting expletive tirade was quite something, even for Geldof. Dylan was not to be put off though. During his set with Keith and Ronnie, he brought up the idea again as Geldof looked as though he was going to have a coronary back up in the TV control room. We love Dylan. And the farmers.

TODAY

One of Jane's books leapt off the bookshelf in our living room today while I was watching the local news. It landed with a thud and there was Jane on the cover looking up at me. I laughed out loud just like we always did in this very room. My spirits rose with hers for a good ten minutes. Maybe half an hour. Doubting Thomas that I am, I need all the books to start flying round the room continuously. But there you go. Of all the 150+ books on that bookcase, Jane's was the one that decided to make that leap. Smile, you dope.

TODAY OR IS IT YESTERDAY?

Money is a strange thing. It kind of made sense back in the Forties through the Sixties. I remember that the Beano comic cost tuppence when I started buying it back in 1946. It was still only threpence by the end of the Sixties. I always bought the Christmas issue. There was something reassuring about it. I don't quite know what it was assuring. It was good to see the Bash Street Kids, Minnie and Dennis still lobbing bricks at authority figures. It was 1970 when my accountant told me I would never have to work again. He should have known better. Just around the corner in 1971 came decimalisation and money never made sense ever again. My annual Christmas issue of the Beano now costs an arm and a leg. It is a fact that a Rock and Roll lifestyle doesn't come cheap. Paul McCartney can still be seen riding the London Tube service. People say it's because he's a man of the people. Bollocks! He's a stingy old git still trying to save the pennies. No doubt he uses his senior citizen pass. Directly before the Daffs made it we were stoney broke. Ten quid between us as we attempted to hitch home after a show. Within a few years our bank accounts were overflowing. Every day we'd check and ever more money was flowing in. As young Liverpudlians we did our best to keep up with the flow by spend, spend, spending. But there was no way we could even keep up. Charities helped. At the first hint of success they were on us like ravenous vultures. Cancer, starving children, the blind, the deaf, old folk, young folk, middle-aged folk, every charity came calling. We gave pretty freely initially until we realised that most of our money was being used to furnish offices for marketing and promotions ratbags. I still regularly check my bank account and am always surprised to find I'm doing ok. Of course, it's now all down to how long I decide to live. The insane ever-rising price of everything keeps that old worry alive.

YESTERDAY

It was 1994 when I met her. Her name was Anne, Annie to friends. I was in Nashville working on my solo album *Women*. Annie worked for CMT, Country Music Television. We met over dinner with Tanya Tucker, Little Richard, Lyle Lovett and Julia Roberts. Also present was Julia's brother Eric but we don't mention him because he's an arse. My album was duets with Nashville's finest female stars. At the end of dinner I asked Annie if we were going to kiss.

'I hope so,' she replied.

As I was at this time living happily ever after with Jane then any right minded person would have to ask the question, why? It's a question that has haunted me ever since. Particularly now. Here are some possible reasons. Not excuses.

1. I'm a Rock star.
2. I'm an ageing man.
3. I'm an idiot.
4. I don't know.
5. Sex.
6. To throw my life into chaos rather than the perfection I had reached with Jane.
7. I'm a fucking idiot.
8. I'm a fucking idiot.
9. I'm a fucking idiot.
10. I'm a fucking idiot.

Back home Jane's shocked reaction was to topple our CD collection from their shelves, go upstairs to our bedroom and take an overdose. She survived. We survived. But we were out of Eden. Fucking idiot.

TODAY

For God's sake! Package arrives in the mail this morning. It's the latest recording by the Bach twins, except they no longer go by that name. They have adopted the name DREAMING DAFFODILS. On the cover of the vinyl they are dressed in full '67 tie-dye crap complete with flowers in their hair. Both A and B sides are covers of our January hit of that year, *Laughing Through the Mirror* and *Upside Down*. I guess they've decided to become a tribute act. I fucking hate tribute acts. The Beatles have about three hundred of the buggers, most featuring a fat Paul McCartney for some unknown reason. God knows what this record sounds like as I found it wouldn't play after I stamped on it many times. Fuckers!

YESTERDAY

It was in the Autumn of 1968 that we officially became Bigger than the Beatles. *Juke Box Jury*'s David Jacobs announced the fact in a column he wrote for the *New Musical Express*. Admittedly, he posed it as the question, 'Dream Daffodils Bigger than the Beatles?', but we took it as scripture. I mean, this was David Jacobs, and he knew a Hit from a Miss when he saw one. We bought up a shedload of copies of the NME that week and had the column blown up to poster size for each of our houses. The actual cutting remains in my wallet to this day. One evening I collided with Paul and Linda. Might have been the Seventies. Might have been the Eighties. We were on the *Wogan* show plugging whatever we were doing at the time. Maybe *Broad Street* for Paul? Goodness knows what for me. In the Green Room before the show I pulled out the cutting to show them. Paul seemed less than impressed.

'I remember David wrote exactly the same thing back in December 1963,' he told me. 'That time his headline was, The Singing Nun Bigger than the Beatles? So you're in exalted company. The Singing Nun and the Dream Daffodils.'

I remember being slightly cheesed off by his snarky response and Linda's giggle. Our egos still flying high after all those years. Anyway, who are you going to listen to, Paul McCartney or David Jacobs?

TODAY AND YESTERDAY

It's nearly Christmas and I find myself dreaming of the long gone past. I fell asleep three times today and these forgotten memories resurfaced.

A PROPER 1940s CHRISTMAS

From age 5 to 7 there was one annual event on my social calendar that I never missed. The Hightown Rugby Club Children's Christmas Party let the festive season begin in the most plumptious way with a grand dinner (with crackers!), carol singing contest (with prizes!) and the arrival of Father Christmas himself (well sozzled). The band began at ten to six usually on the 18th December when we kiddies would arrive in our duffle coats or macintoshes with wooly scarfs, balaclavas and gloves to keep out the Winter chill. The Hightown Club was even more bedecked than us with a huge tree as a centrepiece and miles of glittering decorations hanging from the rafters.

I remember at age 5 being seated next to Appleby, the six year-old convent school bully. He had pledged eternal friendship with me on hearing that my Dad worked for Rowntrees, the chocolate makers. On this particular night, apart from pranging me with his fork between courses, he was in good Christmas humour, happily showing me that he could cram turkey, sausage, jelly and ice cream into his big fat gob all at once. After hitting me on the head with his cracker, he used both hands to tear it asunder. Disappointed with the contents, a pencil, he slung it as far as he could across the room where it hit the local blind girl. From Appleby's roar of triumph, this obviously had made his day.

The organisers were keen to keep things moving at high speed. This added to the excitement of the evening although, post childhood it was revealed to me that the reason for the haste was that Father Christmas was becoming increasingly legless in a side room foolishly attached to the bar. Dinner came to an abrupt end when Appleby was clouted round the ear having been caught smoking behind the Christmas tree. If I remember correctly, he was already a five-a-day-boy by this time. We were ushered into a room with a stage and separated into performers and audience. The audience sat down cross-legged while the rest of us queued up for our moment in the spotlight. My showstopper was 'Oh Come All Ye Faithful' which I performed both joyfully and triumphantly. I was the one awarded a bag of Dolly Mixtures.

And so to the evening's climax. Father Christmas was pulled into the main room on his sleigh by 8 bulky rugby players. We shook the walls with our cheering at this magnificent sight. He seemed very, very happy with a complexion redder than his costume. We loved him and his alcoholic breath. One by one we were presented to him and given a wrapped present (Compendium of Games) and a bag of nuts. I remember him slurring something at me, which was quite incomprehensible thanks to his Northern Irish accent and liquor consumption. Regardless, it was a magical evening and I was a very happy boy knowing he would be making a home delivery within the week.

RAGS - KING OF THE DOGS

That's what I called him. He was a little scruffy boy we found lost on the Dock Road in Liverpool in 1946. The rain was thundering down like never before and he was sat in the gutter, bedraggled with his paw up. We drove on by but Mum's heart was caught and so we drove back. As soon as the car door was opened, he jumped in. No collar. No tags. Pre chips. The police had never heard of him and so the Simon family adopted their first dog.

I was six and our connection was instant. We enjoyed the same biscuits and, on occasion, drank from the same bowl. Rags, for that is what we christened him, and I thought in the same way. We would chase the same things and laugh at the world together. Together - even at school our minds would connect and I'd gaze out the classroom window and follow his adventures around Crosby. Every day at 4pm he would be waiting outside the school for me.

Rags was the fastest dog I have ever known. He could catch the wind. Once I could ride a bike our world expanded ever further as we would speed off along the River Mersey's mysterious pathways. At Christmas times he would always help with the wrapping but he was a lot better at the unwrapping. We had him for nearly six years, which is a lifetime when you are a boy.

One dark day he slipped past me and raced across the road but for once his speed let him down. A ten ton truck was his undoing. He lay in the middle of the road as I knelt beside him and cried his name, 'Rags!' Despite any pain and injury, he gave me one final wag of his tail before his eyes turned heavenwards. We buried him in a corner of the garden he'd loved, and fashioned a gravestone into which we chipped his name and dates and the word LOVE. Say what you like about Lennon, but he got that right. It truly is all you need.

TODAY

I've been asked to give a reading from John Lennon's book *In His Own Write* as it hits sixty years since it was first published. The reading will run in a loop with other celeb readers of his stories and poems. It's for an exhibit at the Liverpool Beatles Museum in Mathew Street. That's the one run by Pete Best's brother Roag Aspinall Best who is quite an exhibit himself. I pick up my old battered copy of John's book and am surprised at how funny it is. Jews, cripples, Nazis and spastics leap off each page. Very 1964 Liverpudlian humour. It takes me back. I find myself wondering if the museum's visitors will find this palatable in this new century and then curse at even having such a thought. This bloody century is getting to me, bit by bit. Go, John, go, anything goes. I will not be editing you, you old sod. Having said that, I choose *Good Dog Nigel* as my reading. That's a piece that could only upset the RSPCA. And all animal lovers, I suppose. God almighty, bloody Lennon!

YESTERDAY

TILL GP, CORONER AND UNDERTAKER DO US PART
By Sir Michael Simon
(May 2024 You Magazine – Mail on Sunday)

Jane and I were in love. That simple fact must be understood for the full horror of the following story to be felt.

We'd met back in 1986, thirty-eight years ago, at Heathrow Airport of all places. Jane was American while I was Liverpudlian. Our love was all encompassing and instant despite the inconvenient fact that she was already married. But we were not the kind of people who would let enraged husbands, US government or Immigration Departments come between us, and soon we were living happily ever after. Our love grew, if that were possible. And then, like a bomb blast, Jane was diagnosed with a brain tumour in 2001. It had grown for twenty years thanks to doctors in both the UK and US disregarding Jane's complaints of headaches as being due to stress or time of life. It was an optician who finally diagnosed the real cause. Operation after operation and radiation followed. And then Jane was put on a daily dose of statins, which ended up having 52 side effects, including a burst bowel. By 2015 Jane's medical history looked like a stack of old telephone directories piled on top of each other. By 2024, Jane was housebound and life consisted of bed to living room chair and bathroom. Having said that, we still laughed every day, including the 21st of January when she collapsed on her way back from the bathroom. 999 responded in minutes but after 90 minutes of CPR, the game was up. Not for a second did I wonder what had happened. At age 74, after 23 years of medical hellish problems, Jane's body finally gave out. Simple fact. The two medics on hand gave me a booklet titled: 'Help After the Death of a Loved One'. Page 1 informed me that the most important thing I must do at once was to notify the DHSS. My wife was still lying on my living room floor as I read those words and tossed the book into a waste paper basket. The medic told me that I would be contacted by the Coroner within three days who would give me next instructions. It being the year 2024, I guaranteed the medic that I knew I would receive no call within that time limit. There was a knock at my door and I opened it to find a policeman who told me his appearance was pure procedure when someone died at home. He told me that he would need to take a statement. His first question was:

'What is your preferred pronoun?'

I told him to have a guess and that I'd be happy going along with whatever he chose. And then I had second thoughts.

'Actually, in your report I'd like to be referred to as the 'Resident Alien'. That was the title on my identity card when I first went over to the US while waiting on my Green Card. In the year 2024, I find the title is more relevant than ever before to my place on this planet.

Two people I can only describe as weirdoes arrived next and told me they were from the mortuary. They had the vibe of those two camp Bond villains from 'Diamonds are Forever'. It took them mere moments before they were handing me Jane's rings and earrings. A strange moment as Jane and I had been drinking tea together a couple of hours before.

Four days went by without any word from the Coroner. Wanting to move ahead with things, I called her up at the number given.

'You are number 45 in the queue. Your call is important to us.'

One hour later, I was speaking to a human being who put me through to the Coroner's Assistant's office.

'There's nobody here today. Please try again.'

Same rigmarole the following day but this time the Coroner's Assistant was in. I asked to speak to the Coroner herself.

128

'Oh no. The Coroner doesn't speak to people.'

Hearing those words I knew this was not going to be a pleasant experience. The CA explained that she was waiting on our GP to sign off Jane's body so that they could instruct me to move ahead with the undertaker.

'I'll chase the GP up today,' she promised.

I had already decided that there would be no funeral as such. I wasn't even planning on being at the crematorium. I didn't like the theatrics of coffin moving along the conveyor belt and closing curtains. They simply weren't Jane. All I wanted was to instruct the undertaker to bring me the ashes, swiftly. I didn't like the thought of Jane still being in a body bag in some ghastly morgue. That evening, a Friday, at five to five, the phone rang. It was the CA to tell me that she had spoken to the GP and he wasn't happy to release the body as he didn't know the cause of death. He claimed he hadn't seen Jane at the surgery in over a year and so was calling for a post mortem. I hit the roof. Under no circumstances was I going to allow these meatheads to butcher Jane. They had cut, probed and prodded her for twenty-three years. Enough! The simple fact was that Jane had been at the GPs surgery three days before she died. She had been in such a bad way that she hadn't been able to make it from the car to the door of the surgery and a nurse had to come out to take bloods as Jane sat in the car. Also, she had been seen at the surgery many times in the past year. A look at Jane's medical history, which had been compared to several telephone directories, would have given a clue as to her death. There's only so much a body can take at age seventy-four.

I hurried round to the surgery, demanding to see the head doctor, a man by the name of Dr Roseberry. I told the receptionist my problem and she disappeared to inform Dr Roseberry. Fifteen minutes later she returned to say: "The doctor says…"

I stopped her there. "You mean he doesn't see fit to come and talk to me himself over this matter?"

The receptionist then said the worst possible thing she could: "He's very busy."

She went on to tell me that he said he hadn't been aware of this problem and thought it must have been a junior doctor who had refused to sign off on Jane. I was told that the doctor said he would raise this issue at the doctors' meeting first thing on Monday morning. I informed the receptionist that I would be there. "That's not allowed," she informed me.

The following Monday morning I arrived at the surgery at 15 minutes to opening time. The rain was lashing down and there was already a queue stretching from the door across the car park. Many old, sick people in that queue. I hammered on the door and it was opened by an officious receptionist who informed me: "You can't come in until 8!" before slamming the door in my face. At 8, I entered and wandered the building until I heard voices from a meeting room. I entered the room and was told I wasn't allowed in there. I told them that I was not leaving until I had told them how badly both my wife and I had been treated by the surgery in the last week. I explained that after 23 years of intense medical problems Jane's body had simply given out and that it was my desire as her grieving husband to get through this bureaucratic nonsense as swiftly as possible. I told them that one look at the extent of Jane's medical records should prove enough to sign off on her body. Dr Roseberry looked me in the eye throughout, a seemingly compassionate look on his face. Next to him stood the head of his management team whose face remained impassive throughout. At the end of my diatribe I informed them that I wanted 3 things resolved that day. 1. An apology from the practice for putting Jane and I though such turmoil. 2. Information as to how the junior doctor involved was to be reprimanded. 3. The release of Jane's body to the Coroner. Dr Roseberry came over, shook my hand and told me: "I will make this my priority today."

Imagine my horror, at 5pm that day when I received an email from the surgery informing me that after due consideration they were not going to release Jane's body and were insisting on a post mortem. No mention of the junior doctor. No apology. Indeed, they finished the email by telling me that if I had concerns in the future to make an appointment. The letter was signed by: The Cumberland House Management Team. No signature. The walls had gone up.

Here is that email:

Dear Sir Michael,

Following your unexpected arrival this morning at the practice and your request for Dr Roseberry to issue a death certificate today, the matter was discussed as a GP Partnership, as well as further discussion with Sefton Coroners Office, and unfortunately we cannot grant your request.

We recognise this is not the outcome you had hoped to receive and can only empathise with the distress you have experienced in the last week. By way of explanation, whilst your wife had a large number of medical problems it was not clear which had caused her unexpected death, and as such this left the GP's unable to give a specific cause of death resulting in the involvement of the Coroners Office.

We hope you can accept this as a final decision from the Cumberland House GP Partnership as a whole. We would also ask that you do not enter a clinician's consulting room without prior appointment to discuss your own personal medical matters.

Regards

Cumberland House Surgery Management Team

I contacted the Coroner's Assistant and told her that under no circumstance did I agree to an autopsy. I suggested that they take a look at Jane's medical records and come to their own decision as to why a 74 year old woman died after 23 years of health issues from hell. In response I was sent a goddamn brochure, a coverall with zero relation to my wife's problems. I demanded to speak to the Coroner herself. "That's not allowed. She doesn't speak to people." Unbelievable.

At 8:30am this Monday morning I was called by the Coroner's Assistant to be told that the post mortem would be going ahead within the hour at Whiston Hospital. I told the assistant that I demanded to be there if they were insisting on butchering my wife's body. "That's not allowed."

I called up Whiston and got in touch with the head of the post mortem team. For the first time since my wife's death I found myself talking to a human being. He told me he would delay the post mortem until I could race to the hospital. Once there, he and a colleague sat me down and listened to my story. He nodded in agreement that the problem lay with the GP's management team. "A not uncommon problem." He agreed that no common sense was in place with the people I had been dealing with. The Coroner's Assistant had told me that if Jane had been 80 years of age, the likelihood of cause of death would have been written off as old age. I had explained that 23 years of horrific medical issues had aged her way beyond her years.

And so, Jane's body was torn apart so these meatheads could have one final piece of paper to sign off on and file where the sun don't shine. The Coroner's office sent me the following report: Jane's cause of death is listed as 1a) Pulmonary Embolism 2) Type 2 Diabetes Mellitus and Hypertension.

Those findings help nobody. The abuse of my wife's body remains with me 24 hours of each day and the fact that I failed her at the end due to these faceless, nameless, heartless and compassionless people.

And then things got worse thanks to the Co-op's so-called Funeralcare. Having explained to their member of staff, Kayleigh, that my requirements were very simple and that I needed no other services than cremation, I was appalled a few days later to receive a telephone call from a head office in

Leeds attempting to sell me various 'special offers' and products that I had already dismissed with Kayleigh. I found it extraordinary that my home telephone number had been passed onto these salesmen to make their money grabbing pitch.

Next, I received via email from the Co-op the most crass, disgusting piece of marketing I have seen in my life. It was a ratings chart like you might find in a teen girls' magazine to rate your favourite popstar; five stars for excellent down to one star for poor. But this chart wasn't for popstars, it was to rate the funeralcare for Jane Simon. They actually used my wife's name on this sickening illustration. When I wrote back to complain, I received no reply. Three days later I walked round to the undertakers to complain in person. A lady in charge of their operation said that she believed it was a very good chart to send to people who might want to review their funeral. I told her such a request was more suited to a pop concert not a funeral. She then offered me a cheap piece of junk urn to place my wife's ashes in. When I asked her why my private email and telephone number were being bandied about inside the Co-op system she simply replied, "That's our policy." I certainly hope that is not true.

I told her she was making things worse and adding insult to injury. She refused to give me names higher up the command system of the Co-op for me to take this issue up with. I've found that in this Age of Communication, such people don't like to communicate. Maybe that's the Co-op's policy. My Coroner and GP also suffer from this complaint.

So what do I want? Simple. I want to attempt to create an outcry so that GPs, coroners and undertakers no longer act in this disgraceful manner. I'm sure I'm not the only person to go through these horrors while grieving for a loved one. I don't want anyone else to suffer in this way. It was all so unnecessary for greed or simple laziness. On behalf of these nitwits who should be going out of their way to help and make the process as simple as possible. After twenty-three years of being a carer for my darling wife, I suddenly had no say in the treatment of her body. That is unforgivable.

YESTERDAY

Speaking of tours, Agent Orange first came into our lives back near the start of this century. All Daffodils had fallen into a malaise of some sort. Nothing really mattered to us. We'd all gone on the peace march against the war in Iraq. Us and two million more, or 45,000, if you believe the Labour Party. In answer to the obvious voice of the people of Great Britain, Blair took us to war a few days later. The most perfect example of a 'fuck you' ever seen. He was soon seen strutting like John Wayne into all news studios to report on the valiant efforts of our boys. 'We must put our differences aside and get behind our boys.' The media tamely obeyed. Our so-called special relationship with the US shone like a fresh turd in the sun. That's when Agent Orange appeared and suggested the Daffodils play a series of concerts in countries considered enemy states by our glorious government. It was a wacky, kind of Liverpudlian idea that appealed to us all at that moment. It didn't hurt that just before her appearance we had been asked to play a Solid Sixties Tribute Tour with the dregs from that period. We signed on with Orange and she did us proud. Dictators from across the world were more than happy to aid us in putting up two fingers to our own leader. They booked us in to play shows in their finest venues and government palaces. Here's the tour schedule she put together:

Hu Jingtao – China
Kim Jong II – North Korea
Taliban – Afghanistan
Saddam Hussein – Iraq
Fidel Castro – Cuba
Assad – Syria
Qaddafi – Libya

Burmese junta – Burma
Fahd bin Abdulaziz – Saudi Arabia
Alexander Lukashenka – Belarus
Khameini – Iran
Robert Mugabe – Zimbabwe
Maaouya Ould Taya – Mauritania
Mubarak – Egypt
Abdelaziz Bouteflika – Algeria
Omar al-Bashir – Sudan
Saparmurat Niyazov – Turnmenistan
Ali Abdullah Saleh – Yemen
Nong Duc Manh – Vietnam
Blaise Campaore – Burkina Faso
Amadou Toumani Toure – Mali
Idriss Deby – Chad

What can I say? It was a pretty good tour and we've not been asked to play a Solid Sixties Tribute Tour since. We played before all of the above dictators and they were, of course, complete arseholes but, say what you like about them, they certainly know how to look after a rock band. Hot and cold girls in every room. It's not Butlins, but then neither is Butlins today from what I hear.

TODAY

I seem to be forgetting things. More than before. I try to convince myself that's because with each passing day I have more to remember but every eighty-four year old's worst nightmare scenario comes to mind with the ghastly word dementia. Merely a home diagnosis as I have the other twenty-first century fear of heading into a doctor's for a proper diagnosis and coming away with Sepsis or some other god-awful waiting room disease. It's all probably nothing and part of me couldn't care less. But then there's the other part of me that dreads the thought of my body plodding on for years while my mind heads off to Bedlam. It's simple words I've known all my life that are becoming increasingly difficult to bring to mind. Pond was one last week. Today it was amplifier. Both words came to me once I stopped thinking. Maybe I just need a teleprompter or idiot cards. Aww, who cares! Because of all this I now have post-it notes stuck all over the place as reminders. The only problem is that I either forget to look at them or can't read my own scrawl.

Today we're booked for an appearance on the BBC's *One Show* to talk about the upcoming tour and album. I meet Laurence and Richard at Orange's office from which the BBC car will pick us up.

'Do you want to go over what you're going to say tonight?' suggests Orange.

'Well, we never have,' says Richard, 'So that would be weird.'

'Have you memorised the tour and album release date to plug?'

'No,' from all three of us.

'In that case just remember to mention that all dates are up on our website, which is....?'

Of course, all three of us were clueless.

'We have a website?' asked Laurence. 'How very 1990s.'

'WWW.dreamdaffodils.com. Couldn't be simpler.'

'Shouldn't the car be here by now?' I asked, looking at the clock.

'You're right,' Orange agreed. 'Give it until half past and I'll call them.'

We gave it until a quarter to when Orange made the call to the *One Show* office.

'The car's not arrived. The boys are here waiting. What? Huh'' What do you mean? Are you joking? When were you thinking of telling us?'

Orange put the phone down and looked at us.

'The interview is cancelled.'

'Why?' I asked.

'Because of a story coming out in tomorrow's Sun.'

'What story?'

'Apparently there has been a string of historical sex complaints about the Dream Daffodils on *Top of the Pops* back in 1975. The BBC is launching an enquiry.'

Richard, Laurence and I looked at each other and burst out laughing.

'Fucking Jimmy Saville rises from the ashes,' gasped Richard, trying to control a cancer induced coughing and laughing fit.

TODAY

The Sun did us proud. Probably because of our Liverpool roots. We got the complete front page under the headline: DREAM DAFFODIL NIGHTMARE and three headshots of Laurence, Richard and myself carefully chosen to capture a look as though we'd just stepped into the dock at the Nuremburg trials. The article continued over onto the first six pages of the newspaper with four of those pages highlighting Laurence;s colourful prison record. The report claims that eight 'young women' now in their seventies have come forward to report on our behaviour at after-show parties held in the bowels of the BBC TV centre back in 1975. One of them, 'Gladys', claims I encouraged her to 'take my top off and suck on my own nipples'. That certainly rang a bell. Actually it rang several thousand bells from that period. Nipples were big round the Dream Daffodils. Richard rang to say he's using the Sun cover as his Christmas card this year.

Turn on the BBC's *Newsnight* in the late evening to find we're the lead story there too except that since this morning's newspaper article twenty-two thousand three hundred and ninety six other women in their seventies have come forward with similar stories.

TODAY

Day six of our trial by the media. All the papers have come in on it now. Front page in most cases. The Archbishop of Canterbury, Lorraine Kelly, Jeremy Vine, Storm Huntley and Tanzi off *Love Island* have all made their opinions known. The body count is now up to thirty-three thousand. The whipped up general disgust seems to come from the way that the media is presenting their prosecution as if we were banging seventy year olds back in our prime. If I remember correctly that was only on one occasion and I didn't hear Mae West complaining when I came up to see her and made her smile. The whole scenario is like something out of *Alice in Wonderland* but at least Alice could wake from her dream.

Richard could finally take no more and opened an Instagram account so he could put our side. Not a good idea.

Richard (to camera): 'Hello. Some of you may have noticed that the Dream Daffodils have been caught in an overkill of promotion in the last week. I'm sure you are as sick of seeing our faces on front pages and tv screens as we are. For one thing, the media seem to be choosing the worst and most menacing photos they can find of us. We're the Dream Daffodils for God's sake. Not Jack the Ripper! Most of our songs were of love and peace. In fact, they all were. Well, apart from *Rape & Pillaging*, but that was for that Viking movie, and nothing Led Zep hadn't sung about before. But I digress, where was I? Oh yes, these silly old bags complaining about being shagged by us back in the Seventies. We were a rock band, for God's sake! We did what it says on the can. Spread the legs and spread the love. Get over yourselves. We have. For those cretins claiming we gave them mental health issues after the bonking, take a look out at the world and find some real problems to go nuts about. In other words, fuck off,

139

Archbishop of Canterbury, Lorraine Kelly, Jeremy Vine, Storm Huntley, Tanzi off *Love Island*, and, most of all, you bleating nitwits in your seventies. Oh, and don't forget to book tickets for our upcoming tour. Can't guarantee a shag after the show though. Love and kisses, Richard and the Dream Daffodils.'

Orange showed me that Instagram presentation on her phone when she called round all in a flap.

'You might want to retreat to your bunker, Mike. Richard is the shit that has just hit the fan.'

TODAY

I used to see sex as the great escape. Turn off your mind and float downstream. All life problems forgotten for those orgasmic moments. Being a widower seems to be quite an aphrodisiac to a lot of women who just want to help and so, of course, I dabbled. Always a big stupid mistake. All I was seeking was distraction from my mind. All I got was Catholic guilt. Typically, after the fact rather than before. I shouldn't really blame the Catholics for that. It's more my own stupid religion of Love. From that there's no escape. Nor do I want there to be. The word you are looking for is 'pathetic'.

YESTERDAY SEEN TODAY

Were the Sixties really that fab? It's probably because of my age that I now find myself arguing against that myth. The curmudgeon lives. If you were to believe the documentaries being made on that period it would appear that it was all about nudity and love, love, love. While the Dream Daffodils certainly had their fair share of love and nudity across those ten years, we seem to be in danger of whitewashing out of memory the horrors of those days that surely stand alongside any nightmares from history. Lest we forget the Moors Murderers Ian Brady and Myra Hindley, the little black girls needing armed protection simply to walk into school, the use of napalm to fry children in Vietnam, the draft to kill nineteen year olds for no sane reason, the greed that created Aberfan's deadly slag heaps, Biafra, and good ol' Charlie Manson and Squeaky. I've never trusted anyone with a swastika carved into their forehead. I could go on but this old man now feels the need to argue against the point he was attempting to make. Yes, the Sixties was as full of horrors as any other decade but, and it's a huge butt, we also had something else that I feel is missing here today in 2025. Something very simple. That four letter word: Hope. Back then we knew we were on route to making a better world. It didn't quite happen. We took a short cut down a cul-de-sac and ended up in this rather hopeless place. I'm glad I'm not a kid growing up today. I don't even hear any protest songs being sung. I mean, where have all the flowers gone? Long time passing.

TODAY

And the fun continues. A hoard of press photographers and film crews encamped on my doorstep. What the hell do they think they are going to capture? A sex mad Daffodil luring in young maidens or seventy year olds to have my wicked way with? This morning the Prime Minister while at a G8 world leaders summit meeting on climate change was asked the all important question relevant to the survival of our planet:

'Prime Minister, what do you think about the Dream Daffodils scandal. Should their tour be cancelled?'

The numpty looked concerned and answered:

'Let me be very clear. These are very serious complaints and need to be dealt with swiftly and rigorously.'

That's going to help, I'm sure. Where's Greta Thunberg when you need her?

This evening a *Britain First* group in Rotherham have organised a Dream Daffodils album recycling skip in the centre of the town. From on the scene reports on *News at Ten* it looks like about ten people turned up with records to toss. Ten people and about a thousand news crews to cover it. Truly, I just hate ...... everything.

TODAY OR MAYBE YESTERDAY

Since the day Jane died it has seemed as though I am living in one unending day. Very unreal reality. Today I uncovered a huge box of our old videos and cranked up the ancient VCR to watch the pair of us plodding around in our old life. We would just turn the camera on and let it catch us sitting chatting over a cuppa with the dog. There was a lot of laughter that didn't translate to today. I almost didn't recognise myself but I recognised Jane and our things. Pictures on walls, nic-naks and so on. I watched for hours. Us, busy doing nothing. Driving to Welshpool. Horses in road. Cows in fields. Music playing on car stereo. Old forgotten much-loved songs. Happiness radiates. Should I shout out a warning of what is to come? Of course not. I love that we are so unaware. An idiot friend of my former brother once suggested I was self-indulgent. No kidding. I've been a rock star since the Sixties. It goes with the job.

Underneath the box of videos was a large old tin dustbin circa Fifties. I lifted the lid and found it was jam-packed with trophies and awards from across the years. Hideously designed tat that had all somehow melded together into one huge monster trophy. Near the top was one I remembered from the Brits or maybe it was a MTV award. I remember that it was presented to Richard and I early this century for a protest song we had written against going to war with Iraq. *Give Saddam a Chance* or something like that. It reached number one in the charts despite being banned by the BBC for 'political and pornographic images in the video'. Tony Blair obviously never heard it. My main memory of that evening is that the award was presented to us by the Gallagher brothers who were in the middle of their own war at the time. As they walked on stage with our award, they were having a go at each other with many a 'fuck' and a 'cunt' picked up by the viewing public. One of them actually dropped the award after receiving a kidney punch from his dear sibling. I can see there is still a chunk missing from the trophy. Ridiculous things, trophies and the Gallaghers. All consigned to the dustbin of my life.

YESTERDAY

December 2010

The One True God came knocking again today in the form of two old ladies. It was a surprise to see Him again as it must be all of three months since He last turned up as two young men in very nice suits from C&A, and I was beginning to think He had forsaken me. No such luck.

"We come in God's name," declared the elder of the two elders, holding up a copy of *The Bible* as proof of her words. "And we bring Good News." I have to say that the Good News was debatable. Apparently there is going to be a purge on mankind. The Bad People are going to be hauled in front of God (and Jesus and the Holy Ghost/Spirit) and finally brought to Justice. And this isn't just the Bad People of today but rather all the Bad People through all Time since records began and possibly even before records began. Now I will admit that there is a part of me that is all for this because I've met many Bad People in my lifetime. That little bastard Ian Schroens immediately comes to mind. Back when we were 10 years of age he took it upon himself to twist my arm up behind my back whenever the urge took him during our time in Junior B. Dead painful that. To this day I would happily see him tossed headfirst into the Lake of Boiling Blood at Level 3 of Hell. The fact that a couple of years ago he tried to make contact with me through Friends Reunited merely adds insult to the injuries I sustained during my wonder years. And then there's the girl who cut my hair two years ago. I send a Plague of Living Scissors in her direction. My own personal list of People I've Met Who Belong in Hell is several yards long. You don't work in the Entertainment World without meeting countless of the buggers. I suppose this is why I wouldn't make a good god. I would allow my personal feelings to cloud my Eternal

Judgment and the vast majority of people I've met in my life would end up Down There.

I asked the old ladies if they thought that the mess the world is in today (a very similar mess to the mess it has always been in) is actually of God's Own Making as he created mankind in the first place. "No, no, no, no, no," said God 2. "He gave us Free Will to choose the Right or Wrong Path in Life." I explained that this is similar to my approach with my own dog, Adrian Monk. The difference being that when he chooses the Wrong Path (a daily occurrence) I don't set him on fire or drown him and all his kin. This information merely brought on a reading from the Holy Pages themselves, explaining that God has the ability to see the Truth or Lie in people's hearts.

We then spoke at length about Life Everlasting and the possibility that that might prove to be a little on the dull side after the first few thousand years. I brought that up, not God. They then offered the Golden Carrot: "Do you not want to see your departed loved ones again?" Well of course that would be nice although again I feel that we would have all had more than enough of each other two thousand years in. I'm great company but there is a limit. I was then given the obligatory Watchtower leaflet: Life Through Death, and invited to a meeting in a church this coming Saturday afternoon.

The Final Temptation: "There will be tea and biscuits." Neither of us convinced the other in our arguments so only Time will tell.

TODAY

The Sun on-line Your Say

Story: SHOULD MIKE SIMON BE STRIPPED OF HIS KNIGHTHOOD?

See full story link.

British Till I Die: Course he should. Needs a good kicking.

Red Dwarf: We should bring back hanging for the whole band and the immigrants.

Rufus Click: Can't read article. Too many ads!

Tiny Dancer: Who cares?

Margery Brown: Why is the story only coming out now? Who covered up?

Russell Garth: Never liked him or his band.

Jimmy Crown: Just watch, he'll probably get off with a warning.

Tracey Brown: He needs God in his life. God will judge him and cast him into the pit.

Ben Fairclough: Awful band. Hate them.

Stan Bolton: Perv!

Vincent Conran: Just give me half an hour with him.

Terry Green: Worst band ever!

Bob Windsor: Nonce!

Jimmy Boswell: Link doesn't work.

Jack Halifax: Knew them before they made it. They were twats then.

Matt Kensit: Make an example of them.

Chris Struker: Never heard of him!

Tony Cutler: Met him once. Up himself.

Martin Downe: He'll be in the jungle this time next year, mark my words.

Vicky Drone: I met him once. He was lovely.

TJ Holmes: Piss off, Vicky! Troll!

Kevin Barton: Kick him out of the country.

John Stride: We need to bring back National Service. The Dream Daffodils should have done two years in the armed forces rather than going into Pop.

Joe Straw: He won't last long inside. Good riddance!

TODAY

BBC NEWS

DAFFODIL ALLEGATIONS GROW

Paul Lynn
Culture Dept.

Sixties icons the Dream Daffodils have reportedly been accused of sexual misconduct by 658,642 men and women who visited the *Top of the Pops* studios back in the mid Seventies. More claims are coming in by the hour say Scotland Yard.

The band's representatives have denied the allegations, telling the Sun newspaper that there had only ever been consensual encounters. Band member Richard Macadam is quoted as saying, 'How the hell am I supposed to remember every shag I had? We were a rock band for heaven's sake. We only did what it says on the tin.'

Back in July the Sun reported the first accusations, which included one from 'Jenny' (not real name) who claimed that Mike Simon had invited her back to his hotel room in March 1975 after a *Top of the Pops* recording. 'We shared a bath together. I remember he was naked. He asked me to sit on his lap. At that point I didn't suspect his motives might be sexual.' 'Jenny' was so scarred by the night that she went on to become a nun at the Ursuline Convent.

Many of the accusers claim that Simon and Macadam insisted on being called 'master', 'sir', or 'your majesty' during sexual encounters. Specific BDSM activities too depraved to mention in detail here on a BBC website, are claimed to have taken place with members of the band without prior discussion or agreement.

Simon's agent responding to these specific claims told the BBC: 'While sexual degradation, bondage, domination, scat, sadism and masochism may not be to everyone's taste, between consenting adults they are all within the law.'

Since the allegations first surfaced, doubt has surrounded the upcoming 2025 world tour of the band. Mike Simon has been dropped from his role as women's rights ambassador in Iran. The release of Mike Simon's autobiography from Bink Publishing is now also under question.

The Tory Minister for Sleaze is calling for a full public enquiry into the Dream Daffodils.

TODAY

Today was the day I realised our game was up. The game we'd been playing since that day back in April 1957 round at Sinnott's house when I saw Lonnie Donegan on the telly for the first time. Agent Orange came round to break the news to me that a local Catholic church group in Rotherham were organising a public burning of all Dream Daffodils records and merchandise. All faiths welcome! Needless to say, the media were getting behind it big time. There hadn't been an event like this since the deep South Beatle burnings back in 1966. All that's missing is the KKK. I used to think we'd come a long way since those days when Lennon was under threat of death for daring to have his thoughts taken out of context by half-witted DJs out to promote their god-forsaken station. But it seems we've merely been travelling in a circle. Makes you kind of nostalgic. Our whole tour has now been cancelled. Venues simply don't want to take the risk of riots breaking out. Bink Publishing have canned my autobiography on the grounds that 'now is not the right time to publish.' A few weeks ago I was bawled at in ASDA by some lunatic holding a can of lager. I now have my groceries delivered by Tesco. A nice old guy who finds the whole thing funny. We laugh on the doorstep. He gets it. Richard was a bit pissed off initially but he's become so feeble that it is unlikely that he would have made it through the tour. There's talk of him going into a home. Ugh! I shall be sure to take my guitar round to play a few numbers just so I can hear his critique, 'Bloody rubbish this! What do they think we are? Kids?' Orange tells me that the Bach sisters have gone back to their original name recognising that the world no longer needs a Dream Daffodils tribute act.

There is a certain relief to knowing we are cancelled. Since those days in the Fifties we've all been on show, always attempting to promote the next thing. Now comes the realisation that it doesn't really matter. Nothing matters. Nothing to write. Nothing to record. Nothing to promote. No need to think. I realise that the tour and the book were mere distractions to take my mind away from my solitary existence but now I'm finding it easier and easier simply not to think. So who needs the hotels and planes and slog of a tour? Time to go. The end is nigh. Bring it on.

TODAY AND YESTERDAY

I would never have described Richard as being sentimental, so it came as a surprise when he suggested a tour round some of our old Liverpool haunts. We sat in the back of his Daimler as it was driven round Crosby & Blundellsands. By Coronation Park we saw two St Mary's College boys in burgundy blazers who we swore were us circa 1957. We immediately christened our driver the Spirit of Christmas Past. This set Richard off on one of his coughing fits. God knows what he was coughing up. A lung from the sound of it. We found Crown Buildings was now Half Crown Buildings due to the passage of time. Sadly, St Mary's was still there. We parked for a good half hour outside what had been the Jive Hive. We said nothing. Just looked … and looked. It all seemed but a moment ago or maybe ten thousand years. We drove on past Merchants Girls and Boys to South Road where this once beautiful shopping area had been reduced to shuttered wine bars or fast food tat.

'I wonder what's on at the Cavern?' asked Richard between coughs. Donning beanies and pulling our collars high, we were dropped outside a Beatle shop at the top of Mathew Street. Arm in arm we staggered along past the Grapes and Pete & Roag's Beatles Museum where a cute tour guide named Jackie was informing a Norwegian party that the Beatle story really began out at the Casbah Club in West Derby thanks to Mrs Mona Best. At the Cavern, the bouncers somehow saw through our cunning beanie disguise and waved us on in with a cheery, 'Good luck, boys!' Neither Richard nor I remembered there being so many bloody stairs. We had to stop halfway down for Richard to catch what was left of his breath. When we finally made it to the bottom of the stairs, the music hit us. It sounded wonderful and we turned and smiled at each other. *Do-Wah-Diddy* of all songs. We made our way through the happy crowd

154

to the front of the stage. It was a very colourful and beautiful looking band named *Carousel*. Three guys and a bird on keyboards and vocals. The boys were solid Liverpool. She equally solid North Carolina. They played song after song, hardly pausing between numbers. I noticed the lanky lead guitarist looking our way and he too must have seen through our disguise. After a word with his bandmates they went into a rip-roaring version of our 1966 forgotten disc, *Shut Up and Kiss Me*. We'd never sounded so good. At the end of the song I turned to grin at Richard to find him crumpled in a heap at my feet. The ultimate show stopper. The medics arrived swiftly and he was pronounced dead on the spot. Apologies to Carousel but when you've got to go, you've got to go.

JUST ANOTHER DAY

Marianne Faithful died today. I was informed of this by the newsagent as I popped in for a bottle of pop.

'Did you know her?' he asked.

Of course we did. Everybody knew everybody back then. It was a small world of music and telly. We all collided. Marianne was jaw-droppingly beautiful on our first meeting in the *Ready Steady Go* studios off Kingsway. It was the third to last episode of the long-running series. She was chatting to Keith Fordyce on set during camera rehearsals that afternoon and looked as though she had stepped from a pre-Raphaelite painting of a medieval princess. There was still an air of the convent about her until we got into conversation in the Green Room where she lit a fag and started effing and blinding with the rest of us. I remember a lot of laughter and common ground as we all put the boot into our Catholic school backgrounds. Like us, she could still recite her catechism. Marianne and Richard got on extremely well and disappeared 'for a cuppa' way too close to going live. Today was Richard's final show at the crematorium. My old Catholic faith makes me hope that he and Marianne are reunited for another cuppa or two in Purgatory or Hell. Maybe Limbo to show how low they can go. Bless 'em both. Bizarrely, Richard's second wife Lucy turned up at the crem. Horrible woman with the looks and fashion sense of Miss Piggy. I recall a line of Richard's the day after they were married in 1972:

'Everything would be fine if she would just learn to shut the fuck up.' Northern Man back in Northern Men times.

Never liked her and nor did Richard so I can only imagine this is the first step in an upcoming wrangle over his will. The show goes on. Sitting here today with this cup of tea and biscuit I realise I know way too many dead people.

TODAY

Well that didn't help. Today the Sun newspaper dug up the following quote from Richard back in 1976:

'I always regret one-night stands the second after ejaculation.'

I'm sure that was funny at the time but here in 2025 it's the signature on our death certificate. We Dream Daffodils are now surplus to the requirements of this century. Truly, as never before, I just hate ….. everything. But, looking back, you've got to laugh.

TOMORROW

Having written this much I kind of feel I might as well come up with a suitable ending to this book despite the publisher pulling the plug. Must be my Virgo instinct needing to finish each project before I can move on. For this book I guess there's no better ending than to pull up my own obituary headline that a friend who worked at *The Guardian* sent me last year. Apparently they have had this on file since I turned seventy-five many years ago. Come the day I hope they use it despite the last few months more lurid front pages.

DEATH OF A DAFFODIL

ABOUT THE AUTHOR

Titanic Tim!...**Stan Lee**

Tim Quinn is good for vibes!...**Brian May**

Genius!...**Gyles Brandreth**

I'll work with them again one day: fabulous people with an enviably generous outlook on life.
Steve Harley of Cockney Rebel on MQM

In twenty years as a teacher (nearly eight as a Head) I can't recall a visiting artist (musical, dramatic or anything) who has had such a positive impact on the children and the school as a whole.
Daniel Hains – Headteacher – St. John's CE Primary School, Southport

Tim Quinn was born in Liverpool in 1953, the very same year Beryl the Peril first appeared in The Topper. Coincidence? We think not! Educated by Irish Christian Brothers whose prospectus boasted, 'We will instill a fear of God into your child', it was little wonder Tim chose a life in entertainment.
Starting his career as a clown at Blackpool Tower Circus he then leapt back in time to work on BBC TV's Good Old Days music hall series where he started writing scripts for top comedians. It was a small jump into the world of comic books where he spent many happy years as scriptwriter, illustrator and editor on such noted titles as The Beano, The Dandy, Sparky, The Topper, Buster, Whoopee!, Bunty, Jackie, Dr Who Magazine, and Whizzer & Chips before heading Stateside to work for the mighty Marvel Comics Group on the world famous Spider-Man, X-Men and the Incredible Hulk.

Tim has also worked as a writer for the Guardian newspaper, editor for America's oldest publication The Saturday Evening Post and producer for LWT's The South Bank Show (amongst others producing a show on the history of Marvel Comics!).

Today he is on a lecture tour of the UK discussing the humour and nostalgia of comics, runs a management company for recording artists, conducts workshops on cartooning and literacy, creates way too many charitable projects, and dreams of the day he will be bitten by a radioactive giraffe so that he can finally take over the universe.

www.ingramcontent.com/pod-product-compliance
Lightning Source LLC
Chambersburg PA
CBHW051141020726
47501CB00005B/1623

* 9 7 8 1 9 1 5 9 7 5 1 5 7 *